ONE AT A TIME

13 Short Reads

Also by the Author

FICTION

Kokang: A Novel of Southeast Asia (2012)

The Defiance of Reiko Murata (2018)

Uprooted: A Modern Odyssey (2021)

NONFICTION

Further Reflections on Things at Hand (1991)

Dragon in Ambush: The Art of War in the Poems of Mao Zedong (with Jeremy Ingalls, 2013)

ONE AT A TIME
13 Short Reads

Allen Wittenborn

Asian Heritage
asian.heritage1@gmail.com

ISBN: 978-1-916820-35-7

PublishNation LLC
www.publishnation.net

Contents

A Soliloquy with the Reader — ix

Three Women in Color — Eastern Europe (2015) — 3

Flight from Iran — Tehran, Iran (2019) — 15

Pedro's Bible — Death Valley, CA (1931) — 39

Li Dan — Guilin, China (1981) — 47

Prelude to Ukraine — Czechoslovakia (1968) — 67

Carla — Los Angeles (1976) — 77

Inheritance — China (mid-19th century) — 107

Field of a Blind God — Burma (2017) — 117

Reiko Murata — Tokyo (1947) — 127

Death on the Yangtze — Yangtze River (1985) — 135

Colorblind — Los Angeles (1963) — 159

Story Behind the Myth — Burma-Laos (1943-1967) — 181

Soulmate — Xinjiang, China (1985) — 195

TO MOE

A Soliloquy with the Reader

I am not a short story writer. Anything less than 50,000 words is definitely not my métier. I'm more of a long-distance runner than a sprinter. So what am I doing offering an offbeat mélange of rather abbreviated writings, none of which is more than 8,500 words?

It's simple, they're in this book because as people do everywhere I like to share what I enjoy. I get juiced up putting words and language in some order to create a feeling or a thought or an action hoping to evoke that same feeling or thought or action into the reader's mind. (Not sure an action can be evoked but I'll let it stand. Call it literary license.)

To avoid calling them "pieces," which is kind of clunky, I will use the standard "story" or "stories." But keep in mind that among literary purists, by and large those with an MFA (Master of Fine Arts) degree, a conventional "short story" is expected to adhere to a certain pattern, although critics scoff at this for being formulaic.

In short, an opening is followed by stuff happening that reaches a crescendo close to the end of the story and then, wham! a climax necessarily followed by the denouement, a wrap up where everything that took place before is brought to a conclusion. Writers like to refer to it as an epitome, the "ah ha" moment when the reader gets it…or not.

These stories don't necessarily follow that formula. A few might but most are something else: vignette, slice of life, account, episode, narrative. Another way to look at these stories is to consider how close to reality they are: fiction or nonfiction or something in between, which itself has a descriptive term, literary or creative nonfiction which describes most of the stories here. In all but two—"Inheritance" and "Reiko Murata"—the story depicts something that took place in real life with my personal input. Hence, literary nonfiction.

Friends have asked me if I embellished any of my writings. If we keep to the original meaning, to "decorate," (literally, "to make handsome") then no, I did not embellish. My contribution was to smooth off the rough edges to make the story readable. This is especially crucial to dialogue, there is no way I could remember all the discussions verbatim that are found here. And as any writer knows, composing dialogue exactly the way a person speaks is as dull as a butter knife. I think I can say that I "enhanced" the story.

A final note. The selections in this collection are not presented in any special order. There is no topic that binds them together, none of them is connected to another. They are not listed chronologically, whether by the date of the story or when I wrote it. There is no geographical sequence. Nothing to do with the number of words or pages. I would like to have some common theme, but there isn't one. They're simply here.

The rest of this monologue provides a capsule description (précis) of each writing. Not to give spoilers about what the story is about, but the reason why I wrote each of them. From where in my imagination were they generated? If that is of no particular interest, then by all means skip them and head straight to the Three Women.

Stories Précis

In **"Three Women in Color"** I may have aspired to emulate W. Somerset Maugham, the famous post-Victorian writer who could be in the most mundane locale, focused on the most ordinary character, and produce a most interesting and insightful story. (Mark Twain was pretty good at it, too.) "Three Women" certainly did not reach that plateau. However, in observing a trio of separate women in three entirely different venues—Istanbul's Ataturk International Airport, an outdoor café in the Greek seaside town of Thessaloniki, and the Ivo Andric train station in Budapest, Hungary—I felt their anguish even though I had not a clue as to what may have caused the anxiety. But the impact for me was a deep level of empathy. Even now, I wonder how each of them is faring.

In May, 2019, I visited the Islamic Republic of Iran for two weeks, one of the most memorable experiences of my life. Yet, it almost self-destructed and this first-person story tells why. **"Flight from Iran"** relates the mad scramble to get out of the country as I stumbled around the Imam Khomeini International Airport with the wrong passport. Knowing not a word of Farsi and afraid I'd be arrested at any moment by Revolutionary Guard guards for being in the country illegally, as so many foreigners had been, convinced me I'd never leave Iran.

The earliest story that I wrote in this collection, around 1990, **"Pedro's Bible,"** is derived from an experience my dad had when he was still pretty young, probably not yet twenty, that he related to me one day. Dad wasn't much given to talking about himself, in fact he was pretty reticent to the point of being completely silent. Drove my mom crazy. "For Heaven's sake, say something!" But he occasionally dropped hints of exploits or episodes he'd been in or witnessed. Like the time in Baja California, somewhere south of Ensenada, when he and his cousin drove an old jalopy down the peninsula looking for work. He didn't recall exactly where, just a little one-street town like the kind you see in a Hollywood back lot. His memory of its detail left him, except he could still see the fast-draw shootout between a couple of guys wearing large floppy sombreros. He couldn't even remember what happened to the two shootists. But my dad never forgot Pedro.

The first year I visited China in 1981 the country was light-years apart from what you see today. Anything that worked was a leftover from the British or the Japanese, the rest Stone Age: rattletrap Russian Ladas or Czech Škodas, bathrooms you shared with armies of cockroaches, hospitals reminiscent of Gothic dungeons. That's in the cities. In the countryside? Rice paddies where xenophobic farmers remained wary and fearful of strangers, especially foreign ones. Stay away from them, not because the government cares, although it might, but because of what society thinks. Don't rile your neighbors. Just don't get involved. All of this underscores my encounter with **"Li Dan,"** at least I think it happened.

I spent the year 1968-1969, summer to summer, nosing around parts of central Europe, mostly Hungary, Romania, Bulgaria and what was then Czechoslovakia. For four of those months, December to April, I witnessed the incredible "Prague Spring," a period of political liberalization and mass protest by the entire Czech population against Soviet hegemony. The gist of this story only obliquely deals with the enemy. What really turned my head and made such an impact on me was to observe the entire populace in a rare instance when the Russians allowed a high mass on Christmas Eve to take place. The people's unshakeable faith in their country and the tenacity with which they fought to save their freedom is indelible. Just blew me away. I originally titled this work "Prague Spring," but given the current state of the world now in 2023, I think **"Prelude to Ukraine"** is more appropriate.

Talk about whiplash. **"Carla"** had me going at sixes and sevens, I mean both the character and the story. It's a true-to-life account that I wrote in the third person. Not sure why I did that. It's possible that I still harbor guilt feelings about the entire business, although I can think of nothing, then or now, to change the trajectory of such a tragic life. Nor was I an innocent bystander. I had hoped to provide help and support to a woman claiming government aid, but as time went on the relationship became twisted, distorted. If you read "Carla," you'll see what I mean. To this day, I can't think of one good result that came out of it, for anyone.

"Inheritance" is only one of two writings in this collection that is one hundred percent fiction, created completely in my own mind, the other being "Reiko Murata." I have no idea what generated this one. Time and place are ambiguous, in this case mid-19th century in central China. The plot is a bit kooky but I wanted a situation where the protagonist gets her comeuppance.

I had a devil of a time coming up with a title for **"In the Field of a Blind God"** until a friend of a friend in New York read the story and suggested this and I found it spot on. Think of it: a blind God. That's powerful. So is the story, not because I wrote it for in a way I didn't. Being familiar with Burma (Myanmar) and Burmese politics, I let it write itself. It's graphic and grisly. It's devastating. It makes you grit your teeth. This account is one hundred percent true.

Everything described in it did take place, not once but many times. Maybe not exactly the way I've written it or necessarily to the same individual depicted here who is anonymous. But these atrocities did happen. I gleaned the details from online videos, journalists' articles, personal interviews, scholars' research, and survivors' depositions. Maybe I shouldn't have included it in this collection, but I had to.

I cheated on this one and excerpted the first chapter of my novel *The Defiance of Reiko Murata*. An editor who reviewed these thirteen so-called stories felt it was good enough to stand alone. It's totally fictional but I based the story on a Japanese film from the 1950s or 60s that I could never let go of. Problem was, I forget how the movie ended, and I don't know the actors' or the director's names, or even the film's title. **"Reiko Murata,"** introduces Reiko, her background, her unique relationship to her deceased husband, and her need to resist the social forces of Japan's misogynistic culture.

Move over, Agatha Christie, you have a competitor. Well, hardly. First, my **"Death on the Yangtze"** does deal with a death but hardly like Agatha's. As far as I know, there wasn't any skullduggery, or at least I don't think so. But after you read this story, a first person retelling of a rather offbeat couple, they're not at all what they seem. And yet, maybe they are. Even so, something seems to be missing. A lot of inuendo and pretense and, yes, maybe some skullduggery too.

How many people in the mid-1960s in the United States dated a person of a different color? I don't mean a fair-complexioned Chinese or a light-skinned Hispanic. I mean an exceptionally ebony Black and a very white White. Even in generally liberal Los Angeles it was rarely in the cards

"Colorblind" features two people who are poles apart in their physical make up, but on the same page in their outlook on life. It deals with a kind of "coming of age," at least for the protagonist who learns something about himself and a whole lot more about the other.

This double-titled work is not meant to be cute or corny. It's because I really don't know the answer. **"The Story Behind the Myth or the Myth Behind the Story,"** is based on the life of an American friend who I knew in Thailand. I've retained the pseudonym "Ty Matson" from my first novel, *Kokang*. Not that it would make a lot of difference, Bill committed suicide on April 1, 2011, which shocked many but surprised no one. Suffice it to say, he left a legacy of derring-do exploits that his friends rallied around dubbing him a "living legend." The work here gives the general background and his elusive role in Southeast Asian history. He was in a way all things to all people, meaning whatever you think about him, you can never be sure. [If you're interested in the real Ty Matson, Google William Young, only after his name add three letters, CIA, otherwise you'll get a hundred hits.]

In leading tours to China, it wasn't unusual to have some bright lights on board, well-known entertainers or social elites. That is, people with money because that's the type of clientele that upscale tour companies cultivated. In my several years as a China escort with Lindblad Travel and Society Expeditions, I met a lot of those bright lights but none nearly as bright as Anita Ellis, a name that most people won't recognize. But if or when you read **"Soulmate"** you'll get to know her. This is my true-to-life account of a stellar figure whom I shall never forget. This memoir reveals her story.

ONE AT A TIME

THREE WOMEN IN COLOR

WOMAN IN BLACK

Istanbul, Turkey, 2015

The Atatürk Airport at 6 am is quiet and subdued. No anxious would-be flyers rushing to their boarding gate. No late arrivals seething when told their bags are overweight. No gnashing of teeth while half disrobing for security checks. None of the busy bustle one invariably experiences.

Only one group shares the cavernous dome. Hearing them speak identifies them as a Turkish family. They are first in line, overseen by a burly unshaven man, mid-50s. This sergeant-at-arms is obviously in charge, hustling about, confirming their tickets, arranging luggage, still an hour before check-in begins.

Whoever he is, Mehmet or Enver or Cemal keeps everyone on the go—four men of similar age Western-casual dress, three women wearing black ankle-length *abayas* and face-covering *niqabs*. Seven people to take care of the other three. And who are they? Two youngsters, say, an eight-year-old boy and five-year-old girl, and the woman, presumably their mother, maybe late twenties, dressed like the other ladies entirely in black but only a *hijab*, leaving her face uncovered.

The children are dutiful and bright-eyed. The boy handsome in a boyish way, the girl cute as a button with her cherubic face and saucer eyes, who delights in playing peek-a-boo behind her mother's garb. The women play a hide-and-seek with the two children who squeal their delight.

Their merriment ends. The woman—their mother?—remains doleful and mute. The little girl clings to her, the boy, more mature, watches her but listens to the men and obeys what they tell him. He is a good boy and is well liked by everyone.

At 6:45, airline attendants arrive for the 9:00 flight. The line has mushroomed in the last ninety minutes to at least a hundred. Four attendants sit down at their stations and open their computers. Moe and I are next in line so should be finished momentarily. Ah, of course, two stations for Business Class, and two for the cattle car. No, make that one, the second cattle woman simply stares at her computer screen and does nothing. This might take a while.

Sergeant-at-arms works the group. Family mills about. "Mother" stands aside as if contrite that her check-in takes so long and looks around at the line of waiting passengers, clearly embarrassed. She squirms when she sees so many scowls. She's uncomfortable, probably wishing this is only a bad dream.

She stands silent and looks around. Our eyes meet. She looks away.

Finally, they are free to proceed to the gauntlet of Immigration and Security lines. She's now without her family, the sergeant-at-arms and his minions can go only so far. The woman seems helpless and distraught, not knowing what where to go or what to do. She's on her own. Moe and I empathize, and silently wish her good luck.

She's checked in and makes it through security. Airport personnel may have orders to desist from checking women too closely. This is a Muslim country. Their passports in order, immigration swishes them through to a large waiting lounge, buzzing and busy. People mingle in duty-free stores, buying chocolates and whiskey. The overhead board of arrivals and departures shows that our flight is on time. Then we espy the trio of mother and kids. I glance at her and she slightly nods in a melancholy manner that I can guess camouflages anxiety and turmoil.

We're on the same flight to London. On the plane, she and her two charges sit three rows behind us. Stowing my things overhead, I look back and smile again. She nods in return. The little girl peeks at me between the seats.

During the flight, I get up to stretch my legs. I notice in her aisle seat she is deep into reading a small book that looks to be in Arabic script, which is probably the Koran. She does not look at me.

Thirty minutes before touchdown, the captain announces our arrival. I wonder what the woman must feel. I imagine that her English is minimal, if any. Maybe she thinks it's an emergency. I hesitate, then get up to give her the message. She doesn't understand me, but the boy does. He relays the information. She beams and clutches the book to her breast. I can see that she wants to thank me, but her lack of English won't allow it. The little girl stares at me with those saucer eyes as if I were a creature from the lagoon.

Our four-hour layover for the London-San Diego flight feels eternal. Sit and watch, roam past all the fancy shops and duty-free stores with useless consumer items that cost more than those outside, giving the lie to "duty free." The airport mall dulls my senses.

Again, we see the trio. I ask her if I can help. She shakes her head, the boy translates, and she shows us her boarding card. She's bound for Houston—as in Texas? We point to the electronic scoreboard to show her the gate number. Her face lights up, then clouds over. Where is Gate C-56? How can she get there? Heathrow is a massive labyrinth of multiple-level corridors and packed waiting areas apparently designed by school kids on a picnic outing. Even locals get screwed up here.

For sure, I don't know where C-56 is either, but Moe and I have time and indicate to her with an array of hand and arm gestures that we will see her to her gate.

Her expression remains indelible in my mind. A look so relieved that I wonder if she'll cry. She does not. She picks up her things, gathers the boy and girl, and follows us.

It's a fifteen-minute trek of escalators, elevators, stairs and an airport train to reach Gate C-56. I can't imagine how she'd have made it on her own. But we all did, and with time to spare. Moe made sure she understood and asked one of the attendants to help her out.

When I turn away, her expression is so full of gratitude it makes me feel guilty. In a babble I do not understand, she again speaks what must be her appreciation. She pulls a hand over her breast in a Turkish show of respect, then goes so far as to touch Moe's arm then mine.

The final scene as we walk away is the woman's relieved face, and the little girl stealing a final wide-eyed look behind her mother's skirt.

WOMAN IN GRAY

Thessaloniki, Greece, August 2016

A warm breeze caresses the alfresco terrace of the Artigioni Café, one of many that line Roxanis Street. Locals and tourists amble past, some in serious conversation, others playfully arguing and laughing, a few, quite a few engrossed in their iPhones. People have pushed aside the country's dire economic malaise, the worst in the European Union since there is nothing they can do and try to enjoy life however they can.

Moe and I pull up two chairs at the small round table covered with a white tablecloth and a blue vase filled with purple and yellow crocus. We scan the drinks menu placed on nearby tables. A young waiter wearing the conventional uniform of black pants and long-sleeved white shirt, sans necktie, asks for our order. We settle on a latte and a "filtered" (plain) coffee. While we wait to be served, we do what one does at open-air dining. Ensconce ourselves comfortably in our chairs and people-watch.

One person we don't see until she appears at our elbows, seemingly out of nowhere is a woman of indeterminate age, draped in ragged clothes, gripping a large plain shopping bag. A dark shirt over a white peasant blouse and a skirt covers her corpulent figure, a washed-out gray-and-black scarf covers her shoulders. Her rough swarthy face marks her as a Roma gypsy, a people reviled throughout much of Europe. In Hitler's Germany, the Roma were as despised as the Jews, and in some cases still are.

I cannot help looking at the woman's dark-complected features. She reminds me of a weather-beaten Apache I once met in Winslow, Arizona. This woman's black-cum-gray hair is tied behind, revealing a wrinkled and craggy face. She wears an expression devoid of emotion, eyes lifeless and staring…at nothing. I doubt she really sees us.

After we place our order, she shuffles over to stand by our table. Not easy to ignore her as she hovers over us, mumbling entreaties that must be asking us for money or some other handout. Silently, we commiserate with her plight. But Greece, nay, much of Europe is so full of homeless beggars that it's hard to keep from drawing a line. We wait stoically for our coffees while she continues to murmur, her hand out, firm but wavering. Moe rummages through her handbag and pulls out two one-dollar bills.

What is she thinking? Where does she "live"? Roma are denounced by most citizens here. I recall the Hungarian family I met in Germany, Laszlo Deszéry, his wife and two sons. Laszlo was fascinated with the Roma conditions and likened it to the Blacks in America. He could be he was off the mark, but at least he understood racism when he saw it.

The waiter comes over to shoo the woman away, which is like moving one of the Parthenon's pillars. I don't know what he says to her, he speaks calmly and without rancor. But whatever it is triggers something, like a veil falling over her. Her countenance takes on a host of emotions: sadness, anger, bewilderment, fear. I can only imagine he is threatening her, nicely for our benefit, to buzz off or he'll call the police.

Her feet are planted, she's carved from wood. Her face, her entire body is rigid, although she teeters slightly as if ready to bolt or pounce or explode. The face mesmerizes me. Like the rest of her, it's carved from oak. A kaleidoscope of feelings seems to rise and overwhelm her. What is she thinking? What is she feeling? Is she starving? She looks robust, a tough weathered woman, but appearances can be deceiving.

Is she afraid of being arrested? Is she married—or coupled—with a man? Has she a family? Does she have children? Is she a druggie? Does she belong anywhere? If she indeed is Roma, then, no, she doesn't.

The waiter again says something. Still, she remains rooted, but wavers, jaw clamped. Her eyes—like ingots of burning coals—stare into space.

A minute passes. Two minutes. Finally, she takes a step, then shuffles off. I watch her wend her way around the tables of imbibers, who take a quick look and return to their kibitzing. She asks for nothing, as if defeated. Her forlorn figure disappears around a corner.

I turn to sip my coffee which suddenly has turned sour.

WOMAN IN RED

Budapest, Hungary, July 2016

Keleti train station. Picture this: think of Graham Greene or Alan Furst or John le Carré to get the mood.

A dank grey ominous cavern with a soaring steel-vaulted roof that rises nearly two hundred feet, heavy with the oily smell of lubricants. One of the major termini for travelers from every corner of Europe. But not at 6:00 am. The chilly steel-lined cavity echoes only muffled sounds from the handful of hunched-over travelers hustling to grab their seats.

We've arrived early to look for the track for our 7:00 departure. But where is it? I look at the large electric board for the Budapest to Belgrade run. I see it identified as the Ivo Andric line. Andric, one of Serbia's greatest modern writers, won the Nobel prize in 1964, largely for his masterpiece, *The Bridge on the Drina*. That doesn't help me much to locate our track.

Moe sits on a bench next to a train bound for Munich. She's watching our luggage while I try to figure out where our Belgrade ride is. We have forty-five minutes and aren't seriously concerned—yet. I've scoured the area, tried asking other travelers. It seems at this hour English-speakers have yet to arrive.

One more turn around the station, then what? I'm beginning to vacillate between self-pity (for missing the train) and lingering fear (for missing the train).

Where is Ivo Andric?

I try asking a glum-looking conductor who stands on the last car's rear steps. She looks, no, she glares at me and feigns her ignorance of English. Maybe, but I question whether an international attendant cannot speak a trifle.

I return to the bench about ten yards behind the last car of the Munich train. The same Miss Sourpuss stands, guarding the last car. Then the final whistle, the last "all aboard", a long-drawn-out wail followed by four quick toots. The conductress in her railway uniform looks around and climbs onto the lower step of the last car. With one hand she holds on, with the other signals the conductor at the front.

The first chug brings a clank of train cars yanked apart, and I watch the woman slooowly being pulled away, off to Munich—

A woman shouts and screams as she races past, the clickety-click of her red spike heels doing double time. She wears a bright red jacket and skirt, white lacy blouse, her hair stylishly coiffed under a matching red beret. She's pulling a valise in her right hand, gripping a water bottle in her left. She shouts at the train, at the conductress, at the world again and again. And again. She's running hard, in her spiked red heels, desperate to catch her Munich-bound ride. She waves frantically, ignores the bottle when it flies from her hand. In her haste, she drops the valise.

Sourpuss makes no sound, no movement. She stands immobile with a vacant expression, like a wooden statue, watching the woman. She makes no attempt to reach out. If she had, there wouldn't be this story.

The woman in red gives one final futile attempt to catch up to that last car. She's yelling and still waving at the figure standing on the lower step, impassively observing the woman's desperate efforts. The train has chuffed a good ten yards ahead, impossible for her to catch as it picks up speed.

The woman slows her running, shuffles a few final steps. She stops and watches the train pull away, takes some time to catch her breath. She returns to her grip, slumps onto it, hunched over, elbows on knees, fingers working a handkerchief, her head bowed, her beret now at a crooked angle. She doesn't sob or wail. She simply sits there, breathing heavily, looking down, ignoring the world around her.

She spreads her hands over her face.

Who is this woman dressed so smart in red? Why was she going to Munich? Visit long-lost friends or family? Start a new job? Meet a paramour? Escape something or someone?

After a minute, she stands, turns, catches me watching her. She gives me a vacant look, picks up her bag, and drags herself away.

FLIGHT FROM TEHRAN

Part 1

Iran, 2019

When I first broached my idea to friends of visiting Iran, their first reaction was: Why? The second reaction was: You're crazy, those guys will pick you up, stick you in prison, and throw away the key. Several people, some Iranian, told him "It's not too difficult to get in, they need the money. It's when you leave that they'll detain you. Be especially careful on departure. And don't talk any politics."

My first response to all this was…well, why not? Not very well thought out, I had to admit. I knew such a venture flew in the face of common sense, and that my friends were right about heading out for a dangerous place full of mad mullahs and unforgiving Revolutionary Guards. My friends were unanimous in their concerns.

And therein lay my reason for following my instinct. I felt compelled to visit this pariah theocracy to confirm a notion I had that opinions people made about a land often came either from misinformation or indifference. I remained convinced that most foreigners held a distorted view of Iran, a place that didn't didn't mean anything special to them. Something was missing. I wanted to see for myself what it looked like at ground level, face-to-face, compared to what the hoi polloi assumed from a distance.

For sure their assessments were spot on regarding the leadership of the Islamic Republic. But my gut told me the experts weren't seeing the entire picture when it came to the other Iran—the real people with the same joys and sorrows and aspirations that I had. The Iranian people were beaten down by religious fanatics, reduced to a faceless and feckless lot. I wanted to remove the mask, to know who these people were and what they wanted.

Then what about the danger of making the slightest misstep, being arrested, and dumped into some dank, dingy cell? The very word, Evin, the name of Tehran's infamous prison, was chilling. Yet acknowledging these possible dangers failed to impress me. Just about every living human is vaguely imbued with the sense that "it won't happen to me." We see atrocities from the outside. Until some dire circumstance does occur, we're safe. Face it, I was a hop, skip, and stumble away from turning eighty which must mean something. That's as deep as my reasoning went. I simply didn't want to address it and put it out of my mind.

The Iranian government required that foreign visitors travel under the aegis of an authorized tour company, Iranian of course. I did an online search, chose an agency named Surf Iran and picked its longest tour, a fifteen-day trip through much of western Iran, including several major cities and a few days in desert oases. In general, I'm dead set against group tours unless I'm leading one. I'd done that in Asia for thirty years. But in this case I had no choice. so I airmailed a cashier's check for $100 as deposit for a visa permit, *not* the visa itself, but an authorization to get one.

Two months later, Surf Iran received the official okay from the Department of Ministry of Foreign Affairs and sent my permit number to the embassy in the US. Not the Iranian embassy, there wasn't one since America and Iran didn't recognize each other. Instead, to the Pakistan embassy where Iran operated a tourist office.

I sent the requisite photo, air ticket, and passport to the Pakistan consulate. Passport? Another no-no. Everyone, including the US State Department, advised against letting your passport out of your sight although State did acquiesce when dealing directly with a government entity. I did the next best thing and photocopied every page, even the blank ones. That done, I sent the envelope with my original passport by Registered Mail, then kept my fingers crossed.

Because America had no financial arrangements with Iran due to US sanctions, the Iranian consulate informed me I had two options to pay Surf Iran the €1900 (US $2200). Either send an international draft to a Malaysian company, Something Berhad (Corporation) licensed in Kuala Lumpur, or go through PayPal. PayPal? Wasn't PayPal, like any other banking operation, also sanctioned? But the payment went through without a hitch. What did PayPal know that Visa or Mastercard or American Express didn't? Six days later, I found my passport with the Iran visa and a receipt for US$ 35.00 in the mailbox.

During the waiting period, any lingering doubts were assuaged by a Surf Iran employee who contacted me on WhatsApp after emailing me. That in itself I thought highly unusual. Again, the lack of reliable information on Iran was staggering. But Sarah's strained English yet mellifluous voice generated a confidence that I was dealing with real people. My more skeptical friends cautioned that maybe I was being set up.

So be it. On May 1, 2019, I boarded my Lufthansa flight to Frankfurt, another Lufthansa to Istanbul, and a third flight on Pegasus Air to Tehran. At that point, I'd never heard of Pegasus. Fortunately I had a three-hour layover at Turkey's immense Atatürk International Airport—named for Turkey's Founding Father—and claimed by Turkey to be the world's largest.

I spent two of those hours trying to find Pegasus. I didn't even know if it was Turkish or Greek. (For some reason, it's Turkish, except that Pegasus was a winged horse in Greek Mythology. Go figure.) Wherever Pegasus was, I couldn't find it.

At 10:00 pm, the airport had emptied and I wondered if I'd been scammed. Was I in the wrong wing or the wrong terminal, or the wrong bloody airport? I imagined being stuck in a deserted LAX or O'Hare. I approached everyone I could corner, all four or five of them, who just shook their heads. Only after I retraced my steps did I stumble onto the deserted Pegasus office: a squat 4 x 6-foot space with a couple of posters, a desk and a chair. I checked my phone and it read 12:50 am, like in the morning. My flight was scheduled for 2:00 am. Problem was, I didn't know if my phone showed the correct time since I was several time zones away from San Diego. I assumed that it did.

I came upon a section of check-in counters. They too were empty, although one of them posted a sign for Pegasus Air, of the winged horse. As if on cue, a few minutes later three agents appeared at the Pegasus, removed the "Closed" sign and placed an "Open" one in its place.

I stood second in line, pushed aside by a grumpy gray-haired matron wearing a black burka and niqab, but without the face covering. Not a problem, the second agent waved me over. In ten minutes, I was ready to go. Checked in my single piece of luggage, hefted my backpack, and felt more than a little excited that I'd made it this far.

My flight landed right on time: 3:30 am. The gods must be smiling. Or smirking.

I'd learned that the Iranian government, probably to increase tourism, allowed arriving foreigners to request their passport not be stamped upon entry in case their own country frowned on such a heinous activity as visiting the Islamic Republic. On the contrary, I wanted proof that I'd been there. When the Immigration officer looked at me quizzically, I pointed to his rubber stamp and indicated I wanted him to apply the full-page seal, signature, and date. The smile.

I was hereby legally and physically in the Islamic Republic of Iran. Even so I hesitated and looked about, concerned that some uniformed official might grab me by the arm and steer me to an interrogation center. Was I still showing signs of American propaganda?

No one grabbed me, no one even paid me any attention. Shucks, no good stories to tell. I retrieved my check-in bag then hit the money exchange, looking forward to the next two weeks meeting and engaging with the flesh and blood denizens that represented Iran's real culture. And from whom I learned that all those messages from TV, radio, and print reports, blogs and podcasts, and the Internet often played fast and loose with the news.

Then the gods smirked.

I entered a spacious high-ceilinged hall lined with a dozen counters, but at this hour only three were staffed: one each for Iranian nationals, Foreign visitors, and officials and aircrews. As fifth in line, I faced the officer in less than ten minutes.

Surf Iran had informed me that one of its guides, a woman named Midia, would meet me on arrival. But she didn't, or I missed her. On the other hand, a woman? Meeting a single American guy? Something didn't smell right. Not only was there no Midia, I didn't find any woman at all. I must have appeared discomfited and certainly and likely made a perfect target. In no time, four young guys approached me from different directions, all offering a taxi to my hotel. How could I know they're for real?

Like a dummy, I asked each of them in turn if they were from Surf Iran. Of course, they all were. In the end, I nixed three of them and settled on a fortyish balding guy who made it plain he'd accept Iranian rials. The others insisted I pay in US dollars or British pounds. For some reason that seemed to show his integrity although I didn't understand the connection myself. So I hustled into his taxi for the forty-five-minute ride to the hotel. Except I didn't know which hotel having assumed that my assigned guide would take me there directly. The driver did his best by stopping at all the major hotels he knew catered to foreigners.

The first two, the Howeyzeh and the Simorgh, were full up and both suggested we try the Amir.

That worked and by 7:00 am I was checked in to although I still didn't know anything about my Surf Iran tour. The clerk said a full breakfast buffet was open on the mezzanine floor. I was its first and so far only guest and sat back to savor the aroma and taste of true Iranian coffee. I poured my second cup when—

"Sir, someone is waiting for you downstairs, in the lobby."

The lobby by now was filled with a dozen or more men, many wearing the Iranian business attire of dark suits and white dress shirts, buttoned to the top, sans necktie. For some reason, ties were deemed unIslamic. The only men wearing ties I assumed were foreigners.

From out of the assemblage, one attractive woman, mid-30s, approached me directly, our first meeting ever, to greet me, apologizing profusely.

"Mr. Wittenborn, I am so sorry for my mistake, but I couldn't find you at the airport," she said thrusting her hand to shake mine with a firm and warm purchase. I was, to put it mildly, shocked. She actually touched me, out in the open where everybody could see us.

I immediately recalled all the horrific consequences in Iran when a man and a woman, especially unmarried strangers, openly touched each other. Totally uncomfortable, I wondered what might happen to me by committing such a major blunder. What might happen to *her*.

I glanced around to see if some Iranian Revolutionary Guard gendarme was approaching.

"Hello, now I recognize you from your visa photo. I'm Midia. So sorry we missed each other," she said, still holding my hand.

How do I respond to that? Fortunately, no one seemed to pay us any attention. "I'm fine, I just hope I didn't cause you too much trouble." Which one of us would the ayatollahs incarcerate first? Such a simple acts elicited barely a yawn in most countries, but here it was downright revolutionary. Single men and women simply did not touch each other, especially if one was a foreigner, and definitely not in view of strangers.

Midia was gracious in explaining that her otherwise unacceptable behavior was within the limits of "official" business. I was delighted.

She quickly, almost surreptitiously had me checked out of the Amir and transported, with my bags to my rightful hotel, the Howeyzeh where we'd stopped and the clerk said it was filled. Turns out I was one of the fillers.

I continued to meet unexpected circumstances. After checking into the correct hotel and making sure my bags were delivered, it was barely nine o'clock.

"You know," Midia said, "the rest of our group, the other three, won't arrive until tomorrow. If you're not too tired, would you like to to see Tehran?" Wow, serendipity.

"Absolutely, I'd love to." I kicked myself for being so enthusiastic, thinking she'd much prefer to be to herself.

"Good," she consulted her watch, "I'll meet you here at 10:30, that will give you time to get organized."

I wanted to tell her I didn't need to and that I'd like to set out right away, but she needed her own rest having been at the airport since three o'clock.

So, my first day in Iran, before the other three of our foursome arrived, Midia and I painted the town red. At least that's what it felt like to me. Just the two of us. My own personal guide. What's not to like.

Midia didn't own a car and apparently Surf Iran had none available, so we took Iran's version of Uber. That Iran had such a service they called Snapp never occurred to me. Not exactly the same since riders had to pay in cash, not credit. Otherwise it did what it's supposed to do with the same security features: car description, license number, driver's name, and cost.

What really really intrigued me was our seating arrangement. Three choices here. Midia sit in the front seat with me in back, placing her next to an unrelated man. Not a good idea. So the foreigner, a male, me, would more likely ride shotgun.

When our Snapp pulled up, I opened the rear door for her to get in.

"No, no, you're the guest," she said, waving me into the back seat. Okay, so she's going to be next to the driver. Brave girl.

When I took a seat diagonally behind the cabby, she indicated I move over. When I did she got in and sat next to me.

Once again I was flummoxed. I wondered if we hadn't gone too far.

"Is this okay?" I asked as the driver entered a cacophonous melee of horn-blowing traffic.

A pixyish smile, "Is what okay?"

"I mean, you're sitting next to me. I thought men and women weren't allowed do that."

"It depends. I'm your guide so of course it's all right."

"You won't get in trouble, I hope."

Midia laughed, shaking her head. "No problem."

"Sounds like Iranian logic," he said.

She lowered her voice. "It's ayatollah logic."

Bemused but delighted, I gave in with no further questions. Not only, we shared the same seating arrangement in all four Ubers that day.

Our first stop appropriately was a mosque, the Emmamzade Saleh considered by locals as one of the city's finest due to its interior architecture. Today was Friday, the Muslim sabbath, so the mosque was chock full—of men, women not allowed, or at least not in the main courtyard. A smaller adjacent hall was reserved for females. I removed my hat and entered the complex laced with shiny pieces of glass that created a glittering mirror effect. Men were everywhere praying, contemplating, paying obeisance to Allah. Many lay about resting or sleeping or watching. No one spoke making it eerily silent.

Too much, I broke out into the sun, a reprieve from the dim gloom inside, but hot and thirsty from the ninety-five degree temperature.

"How about something to drink?" Midia asked.

I laughed. "Thought you'd never ask. For sure."

We headed for one of my favorite venues, a bazaar, think of an ultra-supermarket. Livelier and busy and open to the habit of bargaining that was integral to the culture. I'd seen several in other countries, from Turkey to Burma, India to Kabul, each one with its own personality. The Tajrish Bazaar was typical of most I'd seen complete with all the various and sundry items: fruits and vegetables and meats and nuts, copper ware, jewelry, pastries and ice cream, clothing and fabrics, hardware, books. Midia steered us to a shop that sold an amazing array of fruits and the juices they made.

"Did you ever drink carrot juice?" she asked.

"Not that I can remember."

"It's my favorite. Want to try some?"

"You bet." I found the orange-colored drink tastier and creamier than I expected and ordered a second. "Do they add sugar? It tastes sweeter than I expected."

"Oh no, it's all natural."

As we strolled along Tehran's side streets, Midia came up with another idea.

"Would you like a ride on our subway?"

I didn't know Iran even had one. "Absolutely. How does it work?"

"Much like anywhere else, I suppose."

"Do we go together?"

"Of course. Come on."

To catch the right line we descended five levels, waay down. As Midia said, Tehran's subway was like most others, a subway is a subway. On our ride, I watched the other passengers who also studied me. I said to Midia in a lowered voice, "I'm sure they know I'm a foreigner. You suppose they care?"

"Why should they?"

"I don't know, but haven't they been fed a lot of anti-Western propaganda?" I whispered.

"Oh, they have and they don't believe a word of it. In fact, they're pleased when foreigners, especially Americans, come here." I hadn't expected to hear that. Was she saying it as a public relations trick?

After five stops, we came up for air and spent half an hour meandering through the Abo Atash Park, then onto the Tabat bridge that served as an imaginary boundary for Northern Tehran, the city's tony residential area. A hangout for the wealthy.

By five o'clock, we were both dragging.

"I think we need a break," Midia said. "Let's go back to the hotel, shower and take a rest, and I'll meet you at seven downstairs. We can't do much until then anyway since restaurants don't open before seven-thirty. It's Ramadan, no eating before sundown."

Oops, a big mistake. That meant that a lot of good eating places were off limits during daytime. This is a universal practice in Islamic countries where people are forbidden to eat or drink from sunup to sundown. The daily fast is one of the five pillars of Islam, although foreigners are not usually expected to follow the custom. Even so, a lot of restaurants stayed closed during the day.

When we met in the hotel lobby, we encountered a large crowd of well-to-do clientele that I once again assumed were businessmen and tourists. I wondered if among them anyone was assigned to watch us, or me. Maybe, but Midia and I squared as old friends and set out into the street as if nothing were amiss. For some reason, I could not grasp that such an innocuous act was potentially dangerous. After all, it was well past dark and Tehran isn't one of the best lit cities in the world. Was I becoming paranoid?

We walked several blocks to a rustic-designed restaurant, a downstairs eatery in a four-story building. It was made to look like an old-fashioned farmhouse from somewhere in the Western world. Large wooden beams, tall and narrow doors with French windows, wainscoting, and decorative wall plates. The furniture included roughened wood tables and tall-backed chairs with cushions. Hardly a standard Persian design, more like Little House on the Prairie. Very homey, but the cuisine was local beginning with eggplant, garlic, ginger, and olive oil appetizers. For entrees, Midia ordered seared chicken kabob, I chose grilled white fish from the Caspian Sea.

I studied the drinks menu and realized that Iran is a dry country. Bone dry. The closest to an alcoholic drink, in Western terms, was an array of non-alcoholic beers. I settled for a mildly sour drink made from pomegranates.

My friends in the US assumed that whoever my guide, in this case Midia, was likely a "minder," what you'd experience in Russia or North Korea. Maybe, but in my thinking, a minder never allows his or her charges out of sight for the slightest moment, not even to visit the loo. So…dinner finished, Midia finally admitted to being exhausted, up since the early morning hours nonstop and needed time to prepare for tomorrow's group. When I asked about seeing some late-opening shops, she drew a simple map to show where the hotel was, about fifteen minutes' walk, then politely excused herself. I assumed I'd have to go with her, but she assured me it was okay, take my time and make it alone to the hotel. Again, totally unexpected.

I meandered about without detecting anyone surveilling me. But then, how could I? I put it out of my mind and visited several stores, some like 7-11, others with hardware and bric-a-brac, a pharmacy. Totally innocuous. People greeted me, unconcerned with engaging with a foreigner, especially an American. I was on a learning curve.

The next morning, I met the three others who comprised our quartet, or quintet including Midia. Wendy and Haydn, a retired couple from Melbourne, Australia, and Trish, a middle-aged livewire from Vancouver, Canada. Fortunately everyone clicked. No super egos, no loud mouths. Immediate camaraderie.

From my travels, I knew that the first question locals ask is "Where are you from?" I did it too when meeting strangers. Doesn't everyone? But Iran was now engaged with the US in a serious struggle over so many issues that all boiled down to who was the toughest adversary. Iran dug in its heels on several points in spicy impolitic terms, and Donald Trump responded by sending the Abraham Lincoln carrier task force to sail into the Hormuz Strait. Instinct told me to claim I was English or Canadian or Aussie. No use pushing my luck, especially when I learned of Trump's order in my hotel room listening to my local San Diego PBS radio on my iPhone. I was, quite frankly, nonplussed. How could that be? Wouldn't it make sense for the Iranians to block any and all incoming broadcasts from America?

So when ambling along one of Iran's main throughfares, the Bazar-e-Bozorg in Isfahan, a major cultural center, two young girls I guessed in their early twenties, laughingly asked me, "You are from where?" I couldn't think fast enough and answered, "I'm American," and was rewarded with a most ebullient response. They were delighted that an American came to visit their country. At least, that was the message I took away, one that I continued to receive repeatedly throughout the trip. From then on, I was an American.

Always smiling and eager to talk with me, every Iranian I encountered, men and women and children alike, with that same answer—American—replied with a broad smile and thanked me for coming to Iran. Not only that, they insisted on having their pictures taken with me, so many selfies, even thrust babies into my arms. This open and friendly reception opened my eyes to a world I never expected.

Another eye-opener occurred in Shiraz toward the end of our visit. After yet another delicious Persian dinner, the three ladies decided to have some ice cream. Haydn and I had eaten our fill and begged off to wait outside. We spied a couple of benches near the parlor, one empty, the other taken by a pair of young guys. They nodded when Haydn and I sat down, then continued with their chatter. A few moments later, the chap sitting closest to me tapped me on the shoulder and asked: "Are you gay?"

"Sorry?" I thought I'd misunderstood him or that his English was faulty.

"Are you gay?" he repeated.

This caught me off guard until I sputtered a reply, "No, I'm not." I hesitated and pointed to Haydn. "And neither is he."

Almost with pride it seemed, he retorted, "We are."

It seemed that every day, we witnessed people breaking taboos that I assumed were carved in stone. I came to understand the pressure cooker that Iranian culture had become and *almost* felt sorry for the ayatollahs. Their day of reckoning is approaching, the sooner the better.

Indeed, my time in Iran was an instance of Einstein's theory of relativity that he summed up in his famous quip: When sitting with a girl for an hour it seems like a minute, but sitting on a hotplate for a minute feels like an hour. Iran was my girl.

Part 2

After two weeks exploring Iran's ancient culture topped off by the classic ruins at Persepolis (PER-se-polis), experiencing Persian cuisine, and enjoying its people, we flew back to Tehran to share our final meal together.

For this one, I didn't bother to unpack since I'd be leaving for the airport at 10:00 pm to catch a flight to Baku, Azerbaijan's capital, departing at 2:25 am. I had mixed feelings about leaving Iran. A great experience indeed, but I also anticipated with much delight the trio of Caucasus countries I was headed for: Azerbaijan, Georgia, and Armenia. Perhaps something exotic clicked with me because they were so little known.

During my hotel checkout, the clerk, not knowing who was who in our mix, pulled out all the passports and spread them out on the counter where I took mine. When the other three in the group saw me retrieve my documents, they assumed they'd get theirs at the same time. The guy, a bit ruffled, handed them out but the manager explained the other three must wait until their departure the next day. I remembered the practice that tourist hotels retained passports while guests stayed there. A bit of a kerfuffle with passports passing hands until I got mine and the hotel kept the rest.

As they gave me a hearty bon voyage, Haydn threw in a final caveat. "Just make sure you don't get caught here. I just heard on my iPhone that a couple of Brits have been arrested. Good luck." I promised I'd be dutiful as I grabbed my bag and made for the taxi where Midia waited for me.

On the way to the airport, we chatted it up, discussing the trip and the disconnect between the Iranian people and their government until I espied the control tower lights a couple of miles off. "Here we are, Midia, I enjoyed a great time. You made it that way."

She placed her hand on my shoulder which now seemed like the normal thing to do. "Sorry I can't go in with you. I'm supposed to see you to the entrance but not allowed inside to the security check." We stood slightly apart and Midia held out her hand for one final touch as I slipped an envelope into her hands with a sizeable tip. Well worth it.

I watched the hotel taxi pull away then turned to pick up my things and step inside the modest airport where I'd first landed only fifteen days before. Now, an hour until check-in and I felt satisfied having such a memorable time with good people. I savored the experience.

The check-in counter for my Azerbaijan Air flight opened at 12:20 am, two hours ahead of the departure time. I plopped into a chair in the nearly deserted waiting area and opened my Lonely Planet guide to read up on my next three stops: Baku, Azerbaijan; Yerevan, Armenia; and Tiblisi, Georgia. I smugly congratulated myself in an easy laid-back contentment with plenty of time to laze around for the flight to Baku in anticipation of two more fabulous weeks.

A bit after 12:30, Azerbaijan Air (AA) opened its three check-in stations.

I stood second in line behind a middle-aged lady. The first agent waved her over, while a second, an attractive younger woman, beckoned me. I handed all necessary documents—ticket, exit permit, Azerbaijan visa, and passport. We engaged in some lighthearted conversation as she shuffled through my papers. She stopped, looked up and stared at me with a bemused and then a startled expression and continued to flip through my passport. Without saying a word, she handed it back. I opened it to the identification page. The passport wasn't mine. I held Trish's!

Oh shit.

During the hotel mix-up, the clerk obviously handed me the wrong one, or better yet, I simply grabbed the wrong passport. In my complacent feel-good mood, I'd failed to check it.

Okay, dude, stay cool, except my heartbeat was in overdrive. Flashes of panic flew through my brain, registering all the possible scenarios of being trapped in Tehran, in one of those prisons we all laughed about. Wasn't Evin the most notorious? Somehow my conscious self didn't conceive of anything happening. Which is probably what all those other guys thought who were now languishing in a decrepit cellblock. Is this how they were caught?

Now, let's think this through. What's the best course to pursue here? First call the hotel and explain my problem and they can deliver my passport to the airport. Easy in the US, but a couple of problems here. I didn't know the hotel's number. Nor did I have Midia's personal one. Immaterial since I couldn't connect to a server anyway.

The airport was nearly deserted except for a dozen or so waiting passengers and some maintenance staff. I approached a couple of guys who simply shook their heads. Probably didn't know English or weren't savvy to iPhones. I looked around and found no one else.

I shoved down a feeling of panic that assaulted me, and checked the time, 11:45 pm. I made a final vain effort to work my phone. In the end, I had no idea how to navigate the airport's technology obstacle course.

That left my only recourse, to return to the hotel, get the passport, and hightail it back to the airport. But a round trip under optimum conditions was an hour-and-a-half *if* the traffic allowed. Add to that the time to check in then navigate security, customs, and immigration.

I raced outside wrestling my pair of bags and ran into a couple of drivers who argued over who gets the next fare. Three minutes gone there. I ended up with a scruffy young guy in a scruffier Hyundai. Not a licensed taxi, but I wasn't going to mince details.

Only after the driver, Nuri, started out did I ask him how much. His English was equivalent to my Farsi and gave an answer that was lost in the night air that whipped past us. I didn't care, just get the hell to the hotel. Except I didn't remember the hotel's name, something like "Howizit." I tried to describe it to him. He said he knew it, except every cabbie in the world knows where everything is. The old ploy, say anything to get a trick. If he didn't know, and I sure didn't…a cold wave of adrenalin kicked in.

Visions of being stuck in Iran with no passport or visa, nothing to prove my identity except a California driver's license. Fat chance that would convince a Revolutionary Guard.

I gestured for Nuri to go faster. He shook his head, pointed to the instrument panel where the needle bounced around 80 and said, "Iran." I interpreted this to mean he had to keep to the speed limit of 80 kilometers an hour, or 50 mph.

The Hyundai's digital clock read 11:56 pm.

We reached the outer limits of the city in fair time then faced another problem. A really big problem. Nuri was forced to slow down in the growing traffic. I mean slooow down. The closer to the city center, the more compact the traffic, packed not only with cars but dozens of motorcycles and scooters weaving in and around, many carrying three or four people, shouting and blowing horns and raising all kinds of hell.

Then I realized we were trapped in the middle of Iran's, of the entire Muslim world's most significant event— Ramadan, think Christmas for a Christian. Even worse, tonight marked Eid al-Fitr that commemorates the end of the month-long observance when people are really ready to tear it up. Big-time holiday, really big time. Imagine NY City's New Year's Eve Blowout. At midnight. The one night of the year we needed to break the sound barrier, but the traffic crawled at the pace of a Rose Bowl parade. Everything reduced to a sluggish creep, then stop-and-go, then just stop.

The clock was ticking and we weren't moving.

I still could not come up with the hotel's name, kept trying to pronounce its name and kept coming up with Howizit or how's it. Then Nuri slapped the dashboard and shouted, "Yes, I know it, Howeyzeh Hotel on Taleghani Avenue." Great, but we still weren't moving, stuck in an unbelievably crowded traffic jam. Trucks, buses, cars, motor bikes and scooters, and hordes of pedestrians.

12:26 am and counting. Two hours until takeoff.

Now that he knew where to go, Nuri left the main avenues and tore down side streets not so crowded, though enough to hold them to 20 mph. I figured our chances of making the flight were 50-50 and dropping by the minute. They fell to 40-60 with all the one-way streets that Tehran has a lot of, forcing us to use up fifteen minutes to circle around extra blocks.

12:43 am, still counting.

The Hyundai was still slowing to a stop in front of the hotel when I jumped out and raced into the foyer. The clerk who'd watched me leave two hours before with Midia did a jaw drop. I pulled out the passport and showed it to him. Stunned, the clerk grabbed the phone. Surrounded by three bellhops, everyone immediately started babbling creating a hell of a lot of confusion.

Come on guys, just give me my bloody passport!

I switched Trish's passport for mine and waved to Nuri. The clerk said he needed to contact Midia. A couple of minutes for her to come down. She looked pretty haggard but I didn't have time to commiserate. After minutes of arm-slinging jabber among hotel clerks and busboys and Midia and Nuri, I finally got my passport—really mine after a triple check—and asked her to tell Nuri to get me to the airport ASAP. She did that, then insisted that the forty dollars I offered was too much. Probably, but after three wasted minutes of needless debate, I blew past them and said I'd pay it. I jumped into the Hyundai, waved two twenty dollars bills into Nuri's face and like a shot of adrenalin he put that worn out Hyundai into gear, brodied a U-turn in front of the hotel, then peeled out barreling against the one-way traffic.

12:58 am.

We faced forty-five minutes to the airport under optimum driving conditions but Eid al-Fitr, Ramadan's official ending, was hardly optimum for anything but celebrating.

From then on we swept through the wildest ride ever. Nuri floored it pedal-to-the-metal and we took off a whole lot faster than those bats out of hell. We raced, really raced, sped, tore, shot through nighttime Ramadan Tehran doing at least sixty, maybe seventy miles, not kilometers per hour. Horn blaring, emergency lights flashing. We shot past stop signs which for Nuri no longer existed, who also completely ignored signal lights. In their wake, I saw people shouting and raising fists but Nuri was long gone tearing through Tehran at a mile a minute over curbs and sidewalks, racing against time and traffic. He was hauling ass. I loved it.

"More, baby, more," I shouted.

Nuri grinned, slapped the steering wheel, and pushed that hunk of metal until I knew that engine would explode into smithereens. Didn't matter. I yelled, Nuri yelled and kept his foot glued to the floorboard.

This guy was motivating, driving all over the place, ignoring lane markers and crosswalks, tearing through cross traffic at intersections—the signals be damned—passing cars on both sides. I kept on the lookout and couldn't believe we weren't being chased by half a dozen squad cars, sirens screaming. I thanked Allah for Eid al-Fitr.

When Nuri reached the expressway, he drove *up* an off-ramp and continued to ride the accelerator. We left the city behind and Nuri, no longer holding to the legal sixty mph, pushed that Hyundai until I saw the needle stuck at max speed of a hundred-forty kph, over eighty-five miles per.

1:19 am. No longer counting. Just let her rip.

Then the wait began. That's right…waiting in the front seat where I sat helpless. I knew Nuri was doing his best. But time ticked away, second by second, we seemed to be making no headway, like a treadmill. Nuri was pushing it as if a gorgeous movie star was waiting for him with a bagful of a million rials. I watched the landscape race past but I knew we were still on that treadmill.

Where the hell is that airport? I kept looking for the control tower. Time after time, I caught sight of bright lights and tall structures that turned out to be false alarms. Office buildings and hotels and construction depots.

1:40 am. Forty-five minutes to take-off.

And then, without warning, the engine coughed, the Hyundai slowed to half, the engine still coughing. I glanced at Nuri working the pedal and the gear shift to keep that thing alive. It hiccupped a couple of more times and died.

Out of gas.

We coasted as far as possible, about a quarter of a mile and came to a dead stop. Just ahead, maybe two miles, maybe less, I saw the control tower lights. I switched to panic mode, thinking to make a run for it. But with my bags?

Stuck there, almost within shouting distance of the airport, I knew I'd never make that flight, and no Plan B. Maybe find a new flight the next day, though the Tehran-Baku leg was only tri-weekly?

Those were minor problems. If I got stuck in Tehran, how do I pay for anything? Credit and debit cards were worthless in Iran. Donald Trump had sanctioned all electronic transactions involving US dollars. That left me with a couple of hundred cash. Was that enough to bribe my way out of jail?

What happens to foreigners when they overstay their visa in Iran? Reports were legion of innocent Westerners picked up, accused of espionage, and never seen again. I wondered what the two Brits had done wrong. Other stories confirmed the horrendous conditions in Iran's prisons. What's it like inside Evin? Maybe my friends were right, but what good was that now?

Then I remembered that carrier task force plus a host of Air Force bombers headed for the Persian Gulf. What would the Revolutionary Guards think of that? I envisioned all US citizens, especially ones with no passports, rounded up and stuffed away in some form of solitary confinement, like Jimmy Carter's hostages.

Not to mention that no American Embassy or consular service was available, having shut down forty years earlier. I frumped down in my seat waiting for the police to pick me up and probably escort me to Evin.

1:45 am.

"Hey!" Nuri startled me with a shout and pointed out the passenger window. Unbelievable. Nuri had stopped two hundred yards from a gas station, its fluorescent lighting emitting a bright glow in the inky darkness. Nuri jumped out, grabbed an empty giant-sized soda bottle, and took off at a sprint. Eight minutes later he was back, emptied the can, jumped in. He turned over the starter, the engine coughed into life, and we were off.

1:53 am.

Could we make it? Nuri wove in and out of the sparse airport traffic and jerked to a stop in front of the entrance. We jumped out. I grabbed my backpack while Nuri hauled my larger piece from the rear seat. I gave him two twenties and added a third. We shook hands, did a fist bump, and I raced for the baggage security check where was two-and-a-half hours before. A handful of people mingled about, wishing their goodbyes.

1:58 am.

My patience level reached that of an expectant father who forgot and left his laboring wife at home.

I tossed my bags onto the conveyor belt, then emptied my pockets into a plastic tray. The agent frisked me in five seconds, I grabbed my check-in piece, then…the conveyor belt stopped. My backpack sat inside right behind the rubber flaps. I waited a mind-numbing minute, thought the hell with it, climbed onto the belt and reached in to retrieve the pack. No one said a word, and I raced for the Azerbaijan Air counter.

2:04 am.

Nuri had dropped me off at the wrong end of the terminal. Now I had to double time it from counter 60 to AA's counters 13 through 15. At least a hundred yards. How fast can you run with a suitcase and backpack? Pretty damn fast if you have to. I spun around the corner of counter 15 and saw the area empty except for four agents who stood about, chatting it up.

Gasping for breath, I raced over to check in.

A tall guy shrugged and said, "We're closed." My crestfallen face must have sent a message to the lady who originally handled my fiasco. She smiled and without a word held out her hand, palm up where I placed my passport. She went to her station, checked my bag in, and printed out a boarding pass. Thank God for women.

"Can I make the plane?"

She looked at the wall clock: 2:12 am.

"Maybe."

Ten minutes and I still had to negotiate Customs, Immigration, and Security before catching the airport bus to the plane.

My stomach doing flipflops, I stood in front of a lax don't-give-a-hoot customs official who had no reason at all to hurry. It took three minutes to reach the Immigration section.

2:15 am.

When I saw four lines of people I knew it was all over. Once again, fate smiled. Those four lines were for Iranian citizens. The two Foreign Travelers counters were empty of passengers. I bolted for the one guy sitting in his booth reading a news magazine, shoved the passport and boarding pass at him. He returned the boarding card, flipped through pages of my passport, stamped one, and I took off.

2:18 am.

For the first time in my life, I prayed for a flight delay, maybe just a little one.

I ran up to three officers lazing around and hoped to hell they'd be as casual with me as they were among themselves. They were until one guy asked about my iPhone. Had I taken any pictures? Exasperation. Sure, a lot. I was a tourist for two weeks.

Saying not a word, he held out his hand. I dropped my phone onto it.

The guy fiddled around and obviously did not understand how to work it until I showed him. He scrutinized half a dozen photos and waved me through.

2:20 am.

Where is Gate 12? They pointed and otherwise ignored me. It took me two minutes to reach the departure gate where I had to race down four levels of ramps to get to the bus for transport to the plane, my legs churning like a pair of pistons.

2:24 am.

I reached the Exit door, saw a guy with a badge who pointed to the bus with one other passenger.

"Baku?"

He nodded. Just as I jumped aboard the transit bus, the driver thrust the shift into low and lurched away, the engine growling.

I watched us approaching the Pegasus winged horse, its door still open, the pair of jet engines screaming, anxious to take off. I ran to the stairs and managed to reach the top where I felt like collapsing, struggling to get my breath.

Last on board, I stood there momentarily then made my way down the aisle, heard the door slam, and felt the vibrations of the pushback.

When my butt hit seat 39C, I checked my phone.

2:28 am.

PEDRO'S BIBLE

Death Valley, CA, 1931

Pete's Barber Shop, downtown Los Angeles. A young man sees a sign in the window. "Help Wanted." It's the middle of the Depression, April of 1932, and Pa is long passed. Ma is having a hard time with seven kids. Anything will do.

The young man enters. There is one customer who people called Walt or simply Scotty. Scotty tells the young man about a job in Death Valley.

A group of Chicago doctor barons has just bought a gold mine. They've hired a crew of Mexicans to work the mine. But they need someone to supervise. Someone who speaks Spanish. Someone able to live in the searing desert. Someone who can get the job done.

Some say Scotty is a con man, that there is no gold. The young man doesn't care. All he wants is to get paid so he can help Ma.

The young man is husky and solid. Scotty, too, is a big guy, portly but not flabby. He looks up a couple of inches at the young man.

"Well, son, you think you're up to it. Tell me, how old are you?"

"I turn twenty next birthday, sir."

"A good age. You look like you can handle a dozen Mexes. Think you can do it?"

"Yessir, I do."

"Ever been in a fight?"

"Not much sir. I try to stay out of trouble."

"Good idea. Now, say somethin' in Español."

The young man stands silent and scratches his head. "I can't think of anything to say."

"Well, say that."

"You mean, I can't think of anything to say?"

"Yeah."

"No se me ocurre nada que decir."

"You like Mexes?"

Shrugs. "I guess so, I grew up with 'em."

"I like you, son. You want the job, you got it. Shake?"

"Yessir," the young man grins and holds out his hand.

"Don't you want to know much you get paid?"

"Doesn't matter. Ma needs the money purty bad."

"You'll get fifty cents an hour, the Mexes each get half that. Whenever the temperature goes over a hundred, we add five cents. Sound okay to you?"

"You bet, sir. Sounds just fine…umm, why does the Mexes get only half?"

Scotty ignores the question. "Say, when can you start?"

"Right now, sir. I'm ready."

"Tell you what, I'm headin' back to the Valley day after tomorrow. Can you go with me?"

"Yessir, sure can."

"Good, you'll stay at my place out there until we meet the Mexes. Probably three, four days. Give us a chance to palaver, and get you used to the weather. You realize we're headin' into summer."

"That's okay, heat don't bother me."

"Come back to Pete's, Monday, eight in the a.m. Tell your Ma you'll likely be gone for six months. If it's longer than that, we'll give you a week's break."

"Yessir, she sure will be surprised. Thanks Mister Scotty."

"Don't need a 'mister.' Friends call me Death Valley Scotty."

"Hey, I heard of you. So you're him?"

"In the flesh."

On the drive to what everyone knew as "Scotty's Castle," Scotty did most of the talking. regaling the young man with stories of his background and how he ended up in the valley.

"Ya know, I was once the best shot in the Buffalo Bill show. At a full gallop, I never missed shootin' an ace of spades 'tween a ladies' fingers. I also wrangled most of his horses. He said I was the best cowpoke he ever saw."

"Wow, that's pretty good." The young man paused. "How cum you don't ride with Buffalo Bill anymore?"

"Son, when there's two big men, one of 'em has to go. Can't be both. 'Sides, I thought I could do better on my own. And I have. Located a strain of top-grade ore and aim to pull it out. By Christmas, I figure we'll all be wealthy as a man can be."

"You don't work with anybody else?" the young man asked.

"Just me and sometimes a few cowpokes. But I got a friend name of Al Johnson. We're co-equal partners. He pays me for the work I get done, plus a little bit extra if you know what I mean. We get along quite right."

The next day, Scotty drove the young man out to the site where they'd dig the mine.

"See that small cave up there? That's where you and the Mexes can set up camp. Has a good overhang, use it to build a lean-to, give you some shade. I'll have half a dozen thirty-gallon barrels of water brought in and replenished ever few days. Cover your cookin' and washin' and of course drinkin. Be sure you drink a lot of water out here otherwise we'll be carrying you on a stretcher. We'll also provide food for you and the Mexes and a cook to cook it. You get fodder for the mules, whatever tools you need, and the dynamite. He eyed the young man. "You okay with dynamite?"

The young man shrugged. "I guess so."

"Tell ya what, tomorrow or the next day, I'll have a expert come over to learn you how to work it."

"Yessir." The young man didn't know about that, but he'd make sure he'd learn the learning.

The next day, they drove out to the mine. The young man spent the rest of the day and all the next learning dynamite. Especially important to know how to handle a dud. The only thing you can do was grab the stick and yank the fuse, use your teeth if you have to. Or cut it. But do it fast. The underground heat can cause a rupture making it impossible to get the cylinder out.

Over dinner that night, Scotty explained he had to head out to Los Angeles for a meeting. "In a week or so, I'll check to see how you're doin'. In the meantime, I'll have one of my hands help you build frames for the mine. At least, get a headstart."

With that, Scotty showed the young man his room at the Castle. The young man stood stunned, taking in the sizeable accommodation with a large double bed, white sheets, polished wood furniture, and spacious bathroom and a porcelain tub big enough for three people.

"All this for one person?"

Scotty laughed. "All yours, son, unless you cotton to a young lady to share it with you," he said, winking.

The young man blushed. "No sir, Scotty, I don't figger nuthin' like that."

"Good for you son, keep thinkin' that way."

"Boy, sure wish Ma and the kids could see me now."

When the young man met the group of Mexes, he explained that some of the jobs were harder than others, that they'd all take turns. One team doing the digging, another team sifting for ore, and a third to handle the explosives. Scotty had told him he'd hired a dozen laborers, but one of the men didn't show. The young man said he'd be number twelve. Within a few days, they'd fallen into a regular schedule, a system, wherein each man knew every job.

When Scotty appeared with the first supply shipment, he explained that either he himself or one of his hands would come by once a week to deliver necessaries and check if any ore was found. Scotty at first showed some interest, but after a while he left on another trip and never returned to the mine site. It didn't bother the young man since he'd forged a special camaraderie with the team. Within a week, the Mexes accepted the young man as one of them, and over time, the young man forgot all about Scotty.

It didn't take long for the young man to form a close relationship with Pedro, the oldest one. The young man guessed Pedro to be forty or fifty, maybe more, 'bout what Pa would be. Pedro had no schooling, but everyone appreciated the practical knowledge Pedro brought from experience. What plants and insects to eat, and what not to. How to make a fire the old way with two pieces of wood. Or how to gauge the weather from watching the clouds and listening to and smelling the wind.

The young man also respected Pedro's sense of duty, just as Pedro appreciated the young man's willingness to labor alongside the others. They developed something like a father-and-son relationship.

For eight months, the young man and eleven Mexes scraped, scratched, clawed, dug their way into Death Valley's hard earth. They bored a tunnel at first fifty feet, later a hundred, then more, deep into the mountain, barely large enough for a man to squeeze into with no room to maneuver. They took turns to place five sticks of dynamite in the crawl space. They lit the sticks then had to get out, fast as a jack rabbit before the explosives went off.

After the blasts, thick clouds of powder enveloped the men inside that gave them terrible, nauseous, mind-shattering headaches. The best remedy was to eat the dynamite. The nitroglycerin seemed to help. No one knew why, and no one asked. They just did it. Sometimes they counted only four blasts. Still a live shot in the tunnel. Someone had to dismantle it by yanking out the fuse, just as Scotty had warned. But first they had to get the stick. They took turns going into the tunnel—easy-like.

One day, the old man, Pedro, had his turn to retrieve a live stick. Pedro wasn't well. He was weak and sometimes stumbled. The young man told him he didn't want him to go. Pedro said he should, insisting it was his time. The young man didn't like the idea, but he understood Pedro's sense of fairness. The young man said "Bueno".

Pedro lay face down to enter the tiny opening and wiggled himself deep into the hole to find the dynamite.

The men outside waited, worried about Pedro. For a long time, he made no sound.

The young man called out to Pedro. No answer. The young man had to get Pedro out of there. He entered the adit, then went prone, worked his way halfway down the hundred-foot tunnel. He had to feel his way through the inky blackness since Pedro's hat lamp was off, using his elbows to pull Pedro back the way the Marines did it. He reached out and touched Pedro's boots.

Pedro didn't respond.

The air in the tunnel was noxious, lethal. The young man tugged on Pedro's boots, dragging him from the stash of dynamite sticks. He struggled to inch his way back pulling Pedro with him. When he reached the opening, he dragged the old man from the tunnel into fresh air. Pedro opened his eyes and smiled. He was alright.

Somebody still had to defuse the live shot. The young man reentered the cave. Slow, painstaking work crawling on his stomach. He grew dizzy and weak but forced himself to scrape the hard earth with his fingers. There, he touched the stick jammed into a small cleft, grabbed it, and yanked it apart. But it had taken time. The young man's senses were scrambled, he had trouble moving. But he had to escape the poisonous fumes. He fought to reach the entrance, inching his way backward again, retching until the other workers pulled him outside with Pedro.

Pedro and the young man sat on the ground, gulping mouthfuls of water. They saw each other in more depth. The young man recognized Pedro's integrity. Pedro was gratified at the young man's selfless action.

Pedro had only one possession—his family Bible. It was very, very old, handwritten in pencil on crinkly paper, in Spanish. The date, 1797, was etched onto the cover page.

That night, Pedro offered the Bible to the young man.

The young man was moved. He knew it was Pedro's only property, a treasured keepsake, a spiritual heirloom. The young man could not accept it.

Pedro felt saddened. He placed his hand on the young man's shoulder and smiled. "Entiendo." Then smiled. He got it.

The young man looked into Pedro's timeless eyes, nodded, and thought about Pa.

LI DAN

Part 1

Here's a laundry list for you: Peach Blossom River, Reed Flute Cave, Piled Festoon Hill, Bright Moon Peak, Ram's Hoof Mountain, Fighting Cocks Hill.

I never failed to be impressed with the Chinese penchant to name topographical features, in this case thousands of limestone formations, as if assigning them labels created a kind of ownership. These majestic karst peaks, some as tall as a five-story building, like giant chess pieces, dotted miles of plain surrounding Guilin. Call them what you will, they made for good tourist stories.

I'd been escorting tour groups to China for five years with two upscale American companies, Lindblad Travel and Society Expeditions. This had led to my traveling to every corner of the Middle Kingdom, more than forty cities and towns, including Guilin which is where I'd just arrived for my fourth visit since my initial stop two years before, in 1980 when China was first opening up.

For some reason, this time the town seemed to have changed…but I couldn't put my finger on what that change was. This time the tempo was closer to the beat of the eastern coastal metropolises of Bejing, Shanghai, and Guangzhou. Guilin no longer danced to the tune of a folksy rural backwater, narrow-minded and untrusting of foreigners. From square dances to rock.

"Hey, man where you comin' from?"

I turned to face Gary Downey, a fellow tour leader who often freelanced for museum or professional groups, like the one I was leading here. Gary stood tall and lanky and wore a blond head of hair that reminded me of popcorn.

"Just got in from Chongqing. We're here for five days to study those things with a group of geologists. Of all places to be stuck. How about you?"

"Headin' out tomorrow to catch the Orient Express for Datong," he replied in a soft Tennessee drawl. "Haven't done that one yet."

"At least you'll have a full bar. Lindblad trains have it all. More than I can say for Sleepy Lagoon here."

"Don't know about that, it's pickin' up steam. You gotta check out the Li River's disco? It's a gas."

"The Li River Hotel? A disco? Here? The last time it felt like a retirement home."

"Not now, it's really jumpin' and jivin'. You gotta go. You'll find it on the top floor, where the restaurant used to be. As good as anything in Hong Kong."

"You putting me on, Gary?"

"No way. Ever since Deng Xiaoping took over, China's opened up. Even here."

"I know the major cities have, but Guilin?"

"Every weekend. Today's Sunday, look into it."

"I'll do that. Thanks for the tip, Gary."

After checking the group in and finishing dinner, I turned the group over to the local guide, cleaned up, and made for the so-called "disco." I didn't expect much.

Riding the elevator to the fourteenth floor, even before I reached the top I heard the sounds and felt the vibes of a blowout party. In Guilin? The underarm of China.

I had no idea what to expect but remained skeptical. Exiting the lift, I faced a wall of glass doors hung with white drapes and encountered a couple of tables attended by half a dozen young people handling ticket sales and keeping order. A very simple operation. Except I barely made out what they were saying for the pounding vibrations from the room behind them.

Following the usual ritual of foreigners being charged extra, I handed over five *ren min bi*, RMB, "People's

Currency," equivalent to three American dollars, double what the locals paid, a practice held throughout much of China.

The doorman tore off a stub and gestured toward the entry. I opened one of the double opaque glass doors and swished aside the drapes to step into a cavernous ballroom that could have served as a hangar for a 747. I took a moment to get my bearings and saw a stage at the far end, a light-year away, holding a five-member all-Chinese ensemble: two guitarists, a drummer, a bass player, and a female vocalist. The source of the musical bedlam came from decibel-busting speakers that sounded as if the 747 was inside at full throttle.

Crammed around the other three sides were dozens of tables and hundreds of chairs, some empty of their dancing partners. The only lighting came from coruscating strobe lamps, their garish colors creating a kaleidoscope of painted faces. In the besieged center, well over a hundred packed couples were jammed together, all bumping and grinding to the beat of some heavy metal I didn't recognize. A few couples defied the seductive tempos and simply stood hugging each other to their own rhythm.

This is China, circa early 1980s? Can't be. My brain told me I was deep in Mao country, traditionally xenophobic, with zealous Red Guards going berserk. But nothing of the kind. It felt as if minutes and hours were speeding ahead like a time-warp.

I headed toward a portable bar selling beer and soda, threading through the intermittent spaces that opened and closed to the dancing duos. I reached a point about midway to the bar when someone tugged at my sleeve. I looked down into the pleasantly smiling face of a young woman I guessed in her mid-twenties, but was never adept at reading Asian ages. In an instant, they seem to transform from young to ancient. The sleeve puller sat at a small round table around which were parked half a dozen others.

"Won't you have a seat?" she shouted over the din, gesturing toward the chair.

I hesitated. Her friendly invite rather set me back. Among the several hundred party goers, I clearly stood out, the only white person here and expected to be treated like a deadly virus. In fact, it had taken ten minutes to talk my way into being allowed in at all. Yet, her easy manner eased my apprehension.

"Isn't it for someone else?" I shouted back.

"Please, sit down." She pulled the chair out to affirm her offer.

"Thanks." I took a seat next to her, and noted that those around the table, chatting and drinking, paid little attention. Some nodded and went on with their conversation, indifferent to my presence. I could have been invisible as far as they were concerned.

The music had shifted to Michael Jackson's easy "Rock with You."

"Hello, are you English?" she asked.

"No, I'm not English."

"Australian?"

"No again."

"French?"

I laughed. "No."

"I don't know."

"I'm American."

"Ooh ... I'm Chen Wuling."

"Hello, Wuling. Friends call me Wei."

A pleasant laugh from a cherubic face. "Nice to meet you, Wei," she said, extending a hand that I shook, like holding a feather.

Then something drew my attention to look across the table at a seemingly detached young woman, as if she were the only person present. I stared into the most becoming features: beautiful, pointed sloe eyes, high proud cheekbones, a warm sensual mouth but without a smile, all framed by long silky jet-black hair. All I really saw were those eyes. Brimming with feeling and intelligence and, at the same time, with a deep sense of—what? Anger? Pride? Challenge?

I found her captivating.

"This is Li Dan," Wuling motioned to the woman.

"Hello, Miss Li Dan. Interesting," I said somewhat taken aback since Dan is usually used with males. "And which 'Dan' is you name?"

"Courage, boldness," Wuling still speaking as if defining her friend.

"Of course." I searched for an opening. "Do you come here often?" I asked addressing both.

"Every weekend, Friday, Saturday, and Sunday." Wuling said, just as Gary had told him.

I looked around, watching the strobe lighting circle the room that held, I guessed, two hundred young people, most in their twenties. None seemed to care a whit about this lone foreigner. I turned back to Wuling.

"What kind of work do you do?"

"I'm at the Guilin Museum. Third floor. That's where all the Ming dynasty items are held."

"Interesting. Maybe I can visit some time."

With a surge of bouncy energy, she said, "Oh, I'll show you around. Why don't you come by?"

"Yes, I'd like that. And you, Miss Li? What do you do?"

Li Dan sat at a slight angle which forced her, when she looked over, to peer through a lock of hair that flowed past her eye and over her shoulder like Rita Hayworth or Rhonda Fleming. This, and her natural sensuality emphasized the incongruity of her reply. "I work at the dispatch office."

"You mean busses?"

"Or taxis, or cars. Anything. A lot of tourist business."

I hoped to draw her out from her self-imposed cocoon. "Do you like the work?"

She flicked a lock of hair away from her face. "It's fascinating," she said dryly, as if I asked the world's most banal question, which I had.

Chagrined, I pulled back to address both. "What do you think of the music?"

"I like it, it is so…" Wuling paused to confer with her friends, "so cool." Li Dan said nothing.

Two girls came up and said something to Chen Wuling. She stood and excused herself promising to return shortly leaving me alone with Li Dan.

After an uncomfortable silence I decided to take the next step. "Miss Li, would you like to dance?"

Silence. Immobile. "Alright."

Before I could move, she rose from her chair and moved dexterously through the crowd to the dance floor waiting for me to forge through the packed mass of bodies.

I approached her with a strange presentiment, now unnerved that my initial confidence as a desirable American male was no match for the aplomb of this woman. Her erect posture and lithe figure complemented the fire in her eyes, signaling defiance. Dan also meant audacity.

Moving hesitantly yet intimately to the now fluent sounds of the little combo made it hard to realize where I was, a rural area deep in the People's Republic of China. A wayward settlement that the urban Chinese themselves referred to pejoratively as *xiangxia*, countryside, peopled with country bumpkins.

Still, Li Dan's presence riveted my attention back to the moment in a setting more reminiscent of Tokyo or Hong Kong—or San Francisco, Chicago, or New York. What to make of this, from having a mindset that says rural China is nothing more than peasants, bare feet, dirt floors, outhouses, oxcarts, and no electricity or plumbing? Only vague shadows of humanity flitting across the barren landscape of the mind.

But this is here, and I'm working to balance China's poverty with Li Dan's silent dissent, springing likely from her desire to break out of the straitjacket of the country's suffocating millennial traditions. Is the Chinese peasant, any peasant, an abstraction overlooked by the media and given bare credibility by our imagination? How to reconcile the concept with reality? Besides, Li Dan was tightly pressing her body into mine.

When the music ended, we returned to a table now crowded with several more high-spirited partyers. I sensed that the brief flirtation was at a quick and decisive end. I returned to my seat and made small talk long after Li Dan had withdrawn into the background of conversation. After a stint of discussion with this cross-section of young Guilin, I edged closer to Li Dan.

"Care for another dance?"

"No, I'll be going. It's getting late."

I searched for a follow up. "Can I see you again?"

"Of course, if you'd like."

"Tomorrow night? Maybe we can meet ..."

"Do you know the Chung Hua souvenir shop by the hotel?"

"The one on the corner? Isn't that where Su ... Su ..."

"Su Jungyu. Yes, that's the one."

"I'll meet you there ... eight o'clock?"

"Alright."

The next morning, I begged off from yet another boring "cruise" down the Li River to a dusty hamlet, Yangshuo, an amalgam of peasant huts and tourist shops. Besides, the geologists were focused on their topographical interests and wouldn't miss me.

I set out to explore a site I'd seen in old photos and grabbed a local bus for the two-hour ride to the Ling (Magic) Canal, thirty miles from Guilin, a site little known even to many Chinese and almost nonexistent to foreigners. The site was a must-see for any engineering and history buff. The canal was built around 215 BC by that giant of a man, Qin Shi-huangdi, the First Emperor of Chin—whence "China"—the first leader to unify and personally rule the entire realm. He was also the First Emperor who completed what we now know as the Great Wall, and who commissioned the execution of the famous terra cotta warriors found in Xian.

Talk about a visionary, albeit a brutal one.

In a more practical military maneuver, he ordered his engineers to design an intricate system of channels, locks, dikes and spillways that ran for some thirty-five miles and connected two rivers, fifty feet difference in elevation flowing in opposite directions. One runs north past Shanghai into the Yangtze, the other south into the Pearl River that issues into the Pacific at Hong Kong. All of this to put in place the final link to create an empire-wide waterway network enabling him to transport troops and supplies from the northern capital to the far south to subdue the unruly Yueh tribes, ancestors of the Vietnamese. He succeeded.

My mind was not entirely on history. I felt the day would never end, looking forward to seeing Li Dan. The whole business was quite illogical. Why get all worked up over someone on such short notice? I'd be leaving in a few days and who knew when, if ever, I'd return to Guilin? Forget it. As the Chinese say, you're *yuan-mu qiu-yu,* "climbing a tree to find a fish."

At eight that evening, I left the hotel for Su's store and hangout to find some friends outside on the sidewalk standing around or sitting on a few chairs or benches enjoying the balmy September evening. I'd become a "pal" to Su, who loved the word, not found in the Chinese lexicon, by steering my groups to his souvenir shop.

Li Dan was nowhere to be seen. It was a quarter past eight. I asked Su if he knew Li Dan.

"Sure. You're meeting her tonight, right?"

"Yeah, how'd you know that?"

"I know. She's okay, a good person."

I wondered why Su spoke for her. "Is she coming here?"

"She'll be here."

It seemed that in some inexplicable way, unknown to me, that Su's gathering had quickly paired me with Li Dan. Su kept telling me that Miss Li would show. Then, just before nine, when she did arrive, it seemed that I was supposed to kiss her hand or do something special when she stepped down from her Flying Pigeon bicycle. This in such contrast to what I presumed about the rural Chinese and their reluctance to dealing with foreigners. Yet here I was being openly courted in a backwater corner of China. The numbers didn't add up.

No matter. I was glad and relieved to see her again, especially now that she seemed not so standoffish as the previous night. A slight girl with a pinch of impertinence. As with so many of the young women in China, she combined a cleverly contrived naïve shyness with a dash of Chinese earthiness to produce a most intriguing and enigmatic personality. But still reticent. The little I knew about her, from various accounts, was that she was an accountant at the local dispatch office, and that she lived with her mother, younger and older sisters, the latter's husband, and their two-year-old son. Nothing about her father.

My greeting to her was met with a simple, "Hello," as if anything more was too tiring. She merely stood aside and ordered a cup of tea. I chose to play by the rules and turned back to the general conversation which had to do with one's future in China. The guys especially, but some of the women, too, took to waxing lyrical about how to get away from the drudge of life in Guilin that was so mind numbing.

Everyone agreed that they would do just about anything to leave Guilin and get to the big cities of Shanghai and Peking. I listened to them boast how they'd make it there, Big Time. They were on a roll until their rant escalated into vociferously proclaiming their intent to achieve the ultimate—to go abroad. What this meant, none of them really seemed to know. That and the realization there would likely never be any way to remove themselves from their plight in Guilin, deflated their bombast until they were forced to accept that they'd never be able to change anything.

All except for Su who said he'd stop at nothing to get out. "I'm saving up for it."

"Come on, Su, that'll take several thousand dollars. You'd have to pay a lot of money, a lot more than your student visa plus air fare, much more than anyone can get. Besides, your government wouldn't let you."

"I'll get the money, no matter how much it is. And government guys can be bought off."

"It will cost you at least five thousand US, maybe more."

"I can get ten thousand if I have to."

Braggadocio? Perhaps. But he looked me square in the eye when he said it and I was of half a mind to believe him. In fact, as it turned out, Su had much more money, or access to money, than I had imagined he, or any other young Chinese had. How he acquired it, I didn't ask.

The next day, Su saw me walking near his shop and ran up, out of breath, to ask about changing some money into US dollars. This gave me pause. Did the money come from his business, or some more nefarious activity? Why not simply take it to a bank and have done with it? Su said it was his personal funds, and that local Chinese banks wouldn't change it unless the person presented a foreign passport. Besides local banks didn't deal with foreign currencies. The only place that made the transaction in dollars or Japanese yen was one of the larger up-scale hotels, of which Guilin had but one, the Li River Hotel, where he knew I stayed.

I wasn't so sure about all of this. "What if they want to know where I got the money?"

"They won't, no one cares. There won't be any trouble. Really."

Reluctantly I gave him a tentative okay. He produced a sizeable paper bag that felt like it weighed five pounds, neatly wrapped and tied and handed it to me.

"This is Japanese yen. Take it to your hotel and they'll exchange it for you."

I was nonplussed. "Are you sure? There won't be any problem? What's an American doing with a whole lot of Japanese money?"

"Hey, for sure. You'll be fine. People do it all the time."

"They didn't before. This is the first time I've heard of anything like this."

"You'd be surprised at all the changes going on. It's like a different world. You know, another time zone."

I studied his innocent expression, took the bag and headed for the Li River Hotel. I approached the currency exchange counter, hoping this wouldn't end up in my being arrested or deported—or worse. For one thing, they might want to know how I came into so much Japanese money— two six-inch thick stacks. I had no idea how much it was worth.

I stood in front of the counter contemplating my next move when the female clerk broke into my thoughts. "May I help you, sir?"

"Thanks, I'd like to change some money ... some Japanese yen." I gulped the words down, wondering if I was getting into some contretemps with the local security police.

She remained immobile, waiting for me to do something. "Sir?"

"Oh, sorry." I came back to the moment and managed to hand the woman the bag. I watched her count the bills in the fascinating way the Chinese have. She took on bundle, held together only with a couple of rubber bands, removed those, then proceeded to use her forefinger to flick each bill faster than then a fan at high speed. When she finished, she wrote down a figure, and took a second bundle. When she finished, she wrapped all fifteen into a single bunch.

Without missing a beat, the woman calculated the exchange rate, fingers clicking away on her abacus, and reached for a stack of US bills. I worried she might question the yen or at the very least want to see my passport, but she said nothing. She actually looked quite bored with the whole business of being interrupted to pay out another batch of greenbacks for yet another foreigner. I wasn't about to say anything.

When she handed over the US currency, she asked me to count it to make sure. I was holding twelve hundred dollars. The woman had not batted an eye. I had just learned another lesson: in China a whole lot goes on that slides right past that unbatted eye.

Part 2

I was drawn to Li Dan and met with her nonstop over the next three days. I enjoyed her coy and piquant sauciness, and she was well enough informed that we could discuss subjects other than the innocuous repartee so many young people engaged in.

Still more amazing was her apparent indifference to being with me in the daytime public. Never a hint of any need for secrecy, no indication that being seen with a foreigner was of the least concern to her. Li Dan's nonchalant and forthright manner was even carried to the point of inviting me to her house. That was the last thing I expected and had been told several times it just wasn't done in China. Certainly not in Guilin.

Not one night but three times Li Dan invited me to her home.

At her first invitation, Li Dan met me at the hotel about six o'clock. We walked to her home a mile down a dusty dirt pathway. Sparse electrical lines hung dangling over a cluster of grey concrete block houses, not even whitewashed. I detected an occasional animal less from sight than from hearing: pigs, peacocks, chickens, mules. Very few dogs which surprised me since I knew the Chinese, especially in the countryside, had a penchant for their meat and many farmers raised them for slaughter. I saw no cats at all, maybe they ate them, too. No horses or cattle. And precious few people, at most a dozen on our walk. Were they visiting inside or at work or sleeping? Where was everybody?

Li Dan slowed down and pointed out a nondescript, white-plastered cube like all the others. "That's my place," she said in a flat voice.

"Doesn't matter, I look forward to meeting your family."

"Unfortunately, they don't know English, and little Mandarin."

"What do they speak?" I asked.

"I don't think anyone knows what it is. The locals call it Yongxun, kind of a combination of terms for the two largest cities in the county. It's probably related to Cantonese."

"How are you so fluent in English? It's near perfect."

"Lucky, I guess. I took classes in school and learned the basics. Then when the Voice of America started to broadcast last year, I spent a lot of time learning from it. And I sometimes get English tapes that friends send me."

She stopped in front of the structure. "Well, here we are."

Adult laughter and children's screams issued from inside. I wasn't particularly tall at six-feet-one but had to duck when I went through the doorway. Immediately, the laughing and screaming went silent.

She said a few words which I assumed were introducing me and pointed to a woman I guess to be about forty. "That's my older sister. I won't give you all their names, so hard to remember everyone. Then," pointing to a young boy, maybe five or six and a girl, "her children, twins."

"*Nimen dou hao, wo hen gausying renshi nin*," I tried out my best Mandarin. That brought a burst of giggles, while the four tots rolled around on the floor laughing.

I looked at Li Dan. "I guess I made a big hit with them."

"They're delighted you tried to speak in Chinese. They appreciate that."

When introduced to her mother, sisters and nieces, everyone politely greeted me, and gave no sign I wasn't welcome, always civil and cordial. I had assumed that having an American *yang guizi*, a foreign devil, in their home might cause quite a stir, but it did nothing of the sort. And never did I meet her father, in fact didn't even know if she had one.

Over the next hour in the tiny living room where some of the children slept, I chatted over tea, trying out a few phrases of English, until the older sister called us in for dinner. I wasn't sure of what I ate, but the four dishes were an olio of ginger and garlic and pork. And spicy, I loved it. Li Dan opened a small bottle of the local Liquan beer that tasted like a light lager or pilsner. We drank it tepid because they had no refrigeration.

The next day, I stayed with the geology group, thinking I should show some interest though my mind wasn't there. I met Li Dan that night and she invited me to her place a second time. Since both nights were weekdays the disco was closed and we spent the time together walking along the Li River and surrounding hills that Guilin was so famous for.

On my final fifth night in Guilin, Li Dan invited me over for a third time. The living room, like the first two nights, was crowded with Li Dan's sisters and their friends and children, and other acquaintances who checked in and out as neighbors will do. I tried to communicate but I had little to say and difficult for me to say it. I had to admit I hoped to spend the time alone with Li Dan as we had the previous nights.

Maybe she took a hint from my unease and leaned over to whisper to me, "Let's go to the other room" which turned out to be her and her sister's bedroom. I was rather on edge, not at all certain how this might end up. Yet Li Dan acted thoroughly uninhibited. She simply decided to leave her sisters and their friends to themselves.

That was fine with me, still…

The room was about the size of a small guestroom in a typical American tract home, filled with personal effects and assorted bric-a-brac. Prints and posters of popular movie stars or singers, mostly Chinese, but also Michael Jackson, Madonna, Diana Ross, Bruce Springsteen and several family photos were pinned to the walls. Her furniture included a double bed that she shared with her sister who never seemed to be home, and a rickety bunkbed in one corner stacked with clothes. Also, an armoire, a desk full of books and photo albums, some chairs with various articles of clothing and towels draped over them, a corner set of shelves filled with shoes and more books. A vanity held the usual lady's cosmetics and some jewelry.

I tallied it up. At least seven women and children living here. And one brother-in-law. And they were all only a few feet away.

Li Dan pulled over a couple of chairs and sat down at the desk where she showed me her photo albums, a favorite pastime in China. She said she'd been on the high school swim team as both a sprinter and as a diver. If the photos were any indication, her form was flawless. She had even, for awhile, harbored hopes of trying out for the 1976 Olympics. I wondered about that, but her trim, curvaceous body enwrapped in a tight racing bathing suit was arousing. Was this a trick of some kind, a turn on? Or simply a casual friend showing her high school pictures?

Either way, I was tempted yet hesitant. The room had no door, only a curtain hung in the doorframe to provide a semblance of privacy. They were alone, but not more than thirty feet away half a dozen people were sitting in the living room with a bunch of kids. Almost surreal, with no kitchen odors, no perfume fragrance. Only the scent of a woman.

I tried to read her intentions and came away with uncertainty. Finally, I couldn't resist. Leaning over, I gently tilted her head and bussed her lips. At first, she neither resisted nor responded, but let herself be kissed. After a time, I stood and drew her to me, wanting to feel her whole body. Her eyes, no longer defiant, now wanting, searched mine invitingly.

My mind was scrambled. "Li Dan…" I whispered.

She continued looking deep into my eyes, then gently took my hands and placed them over her breasts. I embraced her, burying my face in her cascading hair.

At that, she pulled away and took my hands. "It's all right," she whispered, "Please," and led me to the bed.

I didn't know what to think. How could they do anything in here? Not even a way to lock the room. But she had already lain down and begun to disrobe. I followed and within a few minutes we lay naked on the bed.

We continued our coupling for a few minutes until we relaxed. Still embracing her, my mind flicked to the moment. I caught her attention and jerked my head in the direction of the living room, silently asking the question about her family. She shook her head in an answer I wasn't sure of, then kissed again, passionately, before slowly easing off.

I dressed while Li Dan arranged herself and combed out her hair. She hugged me again.

"I should be going," I whispered.

She assented, and holding my hand, led me into the living room where several women continued to chat. They barely registered any interest. I said a few goodbyes as I passed through. Li Dan gripped my hand and led me out onto the street.

Again a sense of the surreal. As I walked to the door, I felt like I was passing by a stage play where I remained unseen by the actors.

We stood outside for a few minutes holding each other in the darkness.

"Li ... are you all right?"

"Of course, I'm all right. And thank you."

"Well, thank you. I mean, that was wonderful."

"Yes, it was."

"But your family—?"

"It's okay, we're fine."

"Can I see you tomorrow? It's my last night."

"Of course, I'll meet you on the bridge."

"Fine. At seven o'clock?"

"At seven." She rose to brush her lips across mine.

"See you tomorrow."

The next evening, we met at our usual spot near the Li River Hotel. I studied her, wondering what sort of relationship we had after our tryst. We found a local food stall and ordered a bowl of noodles and veggies, then walked the streets, occasionally stopping or sitting on a bench or low wall. Our conversation was pointless and meandering, neither of us knowing what the future might bring. But I was certain, as I expected she was also, that we had no future.

Even though I had this final night before leaving, for some reason Li Dan did not invite me to her house again.

Maybe it was just as well. Still, I had so many questions about what motivated her behavior of the previous night's affair which did not in any way fit in with my stereotypical view of Chinese social refinement. I had to find out more about what it all meant.

The dilemma came from not knowing if I was now in some way "committed" to her, a custom often found in rural cultures where the slightest indication of interest or behavior between two people could mean a promise to marry.

We stopped walking and I guided her to a nearby bench. She huddled closer to me on the rickety old rattan settee under the cassia tree by a streetlamp, its faint yellow glow casting a pall in the greying mist. We sat quiet for a spell until I spoke and broke the silence.

"Li Dan, how do you feel ... what do you think about last night?"

A perplexed look flitted over her features. "I think it was very nice. Why do you ask?"

"I don't know, I guess it's just not what I expected."

"What did you expect?"

"I didn't expect anything. I mean, I expected that nothing would happen. Does that make sense?"

"Not really. Wei, is something wrong? You look worried."

"No, I'm fine. Well, sort of."

She cocked her head and looked at me with an anxious expression.

"Li Dan, there's something about your culture that I don't understand."

"Oh?"

"Well, does last night mean something? I mean, is there anything between us that's special? Is there any particular reason why you made love?"

Li Dan gave me a quizzical look. "I wanted to. Why else would I?"

"Well, I thought that in China whenever two people make love, it's for real. I mean that it's forever."

Li Dan's smile turned into a pleasant laugh. "Oh, Wei, *ni fang syin*," put away your heart—not to worry. "No, I did what I did because I like you. Why did you?"

"Because I like you too, Li Dan. Very much. I just feel, well ... I suppose I feel guilty."

"Why ever would you feel guilty? About what?"

"Maybe for taking advantage of you."

"You didn't make me do anything. How could you take advantage of me?"

"I thought that you might have some expectations."

"You know, Wei, I read once that in Christian countries to make love to someone you're not married to is wrong or immoral. I don't know if that's true or not, but maybe you're feeling guilty because you believe you've done something wrong."

I had to think about that. Maybe she was right. She certainly didn't seem to be at all bothered by it.

"Wei, in China there are customs that make us careful about what we do. But we can also be very practical and it's okay to follow our feelings, to do what we feel like doing. We can be understanding when we need to be. I don't know what you think, but for us making love is natural, like eating and sleeping. As long as it's done in moderation, and with good intent, and no one is hurt, anything is all right. So, *fang syin*. And if I see you again, maybe we will make love. If I don't see you, then we have something to remember."

When we parted, I did not see her home. Her final words seemed to put a "full stop" to any further discussion. I watched until her figure faded into the mist.

Because of a change in scheduling tour groups for the next year, I did not get to Guilin. When I returned two years later, I couldn't locate Li Dan or any of the friends I'd met. The Li River Hotel remained, but not the penthouse disco.

By 1983, the year after I met Li Dan, China was once again in the throes of a government campaign against *jing-shen wu-ran*, "Spiritual Pollution," the insidious influence of Western, especially American, thinking and practice. It ran until 1985 taking down a lot of unwitting people, especially younger idealistic ones. Like Su. Like Li Dan.

PRELUDE TO UKRAINE

Czechoslovakia, 1968-1969

After completing a six-month intensive German-language course in German in the village of Rothenburg-ob-der-Tauber, I've decided to take the summer to undertake a journey that I hope takes me around the world. First to Asia by car, after that by air. I'm almost halfway there so why not? Well, not quite halfway but the spirit moves me. Besides, my '64 VW hatchback might get me as far as Southeast Asia. Or maybe not. Eh, c'est la vie.

My planned route will take me through Czechoslovakia on my way through the Middle East then to India and beyond. The word among young travelers is that Prague's the place to be. Lively, clean, friendly, good music and world-class wine. I also hear rumors about an impending showdown with the Soviet Union and its seven members, i.e., the Warsaw Pact.

Problem is the Czechs don't much like the Russian bear sitting on them. Younger people are fed up with being told what to do by the unwanted intruders and protesting, calling for more liberalization, i.e., they want their freedom. Events are coming to a boil. In early January, 1968, a liberal ruler, Alexander Dubček, was made Chairman of the Czech Communist Party. He wants to open up the economy and restore individual civil rights thereby flouting Soviet power.

It's August and the "Prague Spring" is at full throttle. It's a heady time and when I arrive early in the month youthful exuberance collides with the ominous signs of a Soviet incursion into a land the Russians insist is a historical and inherent appendage. It all bodes ill in the eyes of the Soviet leader Leonid Brezhnev. Nyet, he makes it clear that such changes are not to be.

And so, on the fateful day of August 20, 1968, I cross the border in my little VW and drive to Karlovy Vary, noted for its hot springs, not realizing that "hot springs" could be a euphemism for what's happening now. I continue driving through the rolling wheat fields of the Czech countryside. But instead of a scenic tour expecting to see peasants preparing for the next crop, I see people running helter-skelter under dark clouds that turn out to be man-made evidence of artillery cannonades. Word spreads quickly of invasion and war. At first I wasn't convinced and believed that such whispers were merely rumors. But the growing testimony of hostilities soon overturn my skepticism.

Barely days after the Russians rolled across the border and through Czech woods and farmland, there is little visible evidence of the invasion, but the takeover is thorough. In only one week, Russian tanks crushed Czech leader Alexander Dubček's political and economic reforms that he hoped would enable his country to slip away from the grip of the powerful Soviet Union. But the Kremlin had other ideas and refused to allow any dissent or free thinking under its jackboots and launched a withering blitzkrieg.

It takes me three days to reach Prague instead of the single-day trip I had calculated. Initially, I didn't witness any active combat operations but the closer I get to the capital the more evidence I see of how Warsaw Pact troops have sewn destruction in town and country in a lightning-swift move to stamp out the search for independence: mangled jeeps clogging country roads, buildings pockmarked by bullets and shrapnel, smashed cannons rusting in scorched fields. Then signs of scattered resistance: highway signs painted over meant to direct traffic to Moscow, young people assaulting police and soldiers in hit-and-run tactics, defiant acts of self-immolation leave the air reeking with the smell of burnt flesh. In the end, Brezhnev's hordes easily overwhelmed the country's meager if spirited resistance.

Once in Prague I search for a place to stay. A group of college students steers me to the Hotel King George that easily fit the description of "a cozy hotel with a charming restaurant…a quaint historical accommodation dating back to the 14th century," conveniently located on Prague's central Wenceslaus Square.

I take to the hotel manager, a kindly if stern gentleman with the old country sense of propriety. Possibly born into wealth and plenty that had been ground down first by Nazi, then Russian oppression. His leathery face belies his not so many years, about my own father's fifty something. Josef Kolmas treats me with a special decorum, almost as if I'm a long-lost son. By the third day, we've struck up a close relationship.

"I think you are maybe about Robert's age, my son. He will be here in two or three days. Maybe you can meet, yes?"

"Yessir, Mr. Kolmas. I look forward—"

"Ah, not Mister, no more of that. It's Yosef, Yosef with a J. You will meet Robert. He will show you the city, take you to Hradcany Castle. You will see."

"Very well, Yosef with a J. Maybe we can meet here at the hotel."

"Yes, of course. That is good. I will let you know when he is here."

Robert Kolmas returns at once from England where he studies economics. He exudes enthusiasm and energy, yet feels helpless. "I must be here. This is my place, these are my people. Those damned Russians and their lackies."

"I get it. I'd like to do whatever I can to help."

"Let's see what we can do about that. How about going to the university tomorrow. I'll introduce you to my friends, angry like me."

"Yes, I'd like that."

The next day, Robert grabs a taxi and takes me to Charles University's Union Club to meet the students, in fact the entire student body, who denounce Russian hegemony, sing anti-Russian songs, string up banners denouncing Moscow's minions. And I can feel their fear and anger hidden behind the gaiety.

EASTER EGG COLORING.

A week into the invasion and students, male and female, are dropping out of school to fight for the cause. taking part in any way they can. Some join the army, others volunteer as mechanics or repairmen. Still others turn to the medical and health services, or public safety and fire control. Their talk and promises to lash out reach hyperbolic levels. I see it in Robert's vehemence, but he will not be reconciled. He purveyed the sense of outrage of all Czechs.

She might have invaded Russia.

"I detest the Russian arrogance and propoganda and their simple talk that this is for our good. Or that it's only right that the Soviet Union reclaim or retain what rightfully belongs to it. I don't know if the leaders really believe all their bullshit, but they make sure the Russian people do. Those bastards"!

Robert's father, Josef, is just as outraged, but more circumspect. He's been there. He fought in the underground against the Nazis. He was wounded, captured, and tortured, scarred for life. He speaks seven languages and works at the hotel.

"Robert, you can't do anything now. Wait and work and believe in your country, yes of course. But don't throw away your life on such trash. Trust your leaders and the people."

"But Papa, we have to show them we won't just lie down. We must fight. Hope and faith are not enough."

"In time, Robert, in time."

"Papa, time is not on our side," Robert pleads with the older man.

Robert and his father disagree on how to deal with the invasion, but they both reflect the people's emotions. All of Czechoslovakia combines the heated frustration and tempered discretion of son and father. They agree that the citizenry must do as little as possible to obey the Russian overlords, for the Czech people are spirited and unyielding.

"We will never give up!" Robert asserts, smashing a fist into his palm.

But Czechs also know their limitations. Guns and bullets have no match. Newsmen around the world report the story, yet the pen is not always mightier than the sword. Still, nothing can kill a belief.

I delay my self-imposed departure, reluctant to leave these courageous, tenacious people. I hang out with Robert and his friends who introduce me to meet professors, talk to shopkeepers, listen to taxi drivers, mingle with people on the street.

After a week by which time the Russian-led forces are ensconced and in complete control, Robert invites me to go with him to visit his grandmama, Josef's mother. She lives in the south, in Çeske Budejoviçe, known under the Nazis as Budweis, a town on the way to Vienna. Granmama

Chermakova is a spry impatient woman of eighty who hates the people who tramp her land. First the Austro-Hungarians, then the Germans, now the Russians. She fought against them all, but the Russians she hates most of all.

"The Russkies, *smilníci*, whoremasters." She spits. "They pretend to be friends, that they want to help you. Like the Nazis, they are not human, worse than animals. They are odious filth. They are shit!" The old woman fumes, but she takes heart in her grandson, the future of her people during this holy season. The aged woman, her hair sprigs of grey, pulls back and smiles, looking at me. "And you, young man, you say your grandmother, too, was named Elizabeth. When I was young, my family called me Alžběta, so she is my namesake."

Grandmama's comment touches me. In only a few days, I've become connected to the Czech people, and now this old woman has brought me into the inner orbit of Czech society. I feel at home here and avidly accept when Robert asks me to go with him and friends to attend a midnight mass back in Prague. Though I'm not Catholic, or even Christian for that matter, I jump at the invitation.

"You know, this is the first Christian celebration allowed in *twenty years*. That's when the Communists snuffed out our freedom to worship, like pinching a candle flame. After all this time, we can congregate to practice our belief."

It seems the Russkies, having imposed their control over the country, in their arrogance feel they can unlock the portal to freedom. For now, Dubček is free and the church door stands open.

The entire city is on a high, an almost intoxicating sense of expectation hones the senses to a razor-sharp edge for the midnight high mass. We reach the church at nine-thirty, already packed with hundreds waiting in the courtyard. At least several hundred people inside, no, a thousand—maybe more.

I manage to squeeze my way into the interior and find an entire cathedral so packed there is simply no place to move, elbow to elbow. Old grannies—so many like Alžběta—in black shawls and kerchiefs, young children dressed in neat homemade jumpers, middle-aged lawyers and accountants in drab suits and ties, wives in colorful skirts and blouses and jackets, teenagers with jeans and long hair, workers in rough dungarees and overalls, young ladies wearing cheap fur coats, office workers, street sweepers, professors, farmers, bureaucrats, actors, soldiers, doctors, musicians. An entire cross-section of Czech society.

Eleven o'clock. A hushed expectancy infuses the area, an impatience heightened by anticipation. These people can be rounded up at any moment, checked by KGB thugs, and hauled off to anonymity, never to be heard from again. But they stay, choosing to express their convictions in the only way they can—through the act of worship.

They are vulnerable, but they will not cave.

Eleven-thirty. A child whimpers, is shushed by its mother. Noises outside—the stomp of heels on cobblestone. Everyone tenses, praying for just a little while longer this qualified freedom.

Faces taut, parents hug tight their children, and each other.

The trample of jackboots passes.

A single inaudible sigh.

Eleven forty-five. A restlessness spurs these people into defiance. Eyes raise, looking for the priest, searching for God. At ten minutes to twelve, a bishop enters, ascends the dais, greeted by a deep well of silent thanks. It is perceptible, this silence. The bishop begins to intone a mass. Some people bow their heads, eyes clamped shut. Others, hoping to inhale every drop of this incomparable happening, gaze about in wonderment.

"I love God, God is my Savior, the church is my refuge. Please Russians go away, let us pray and love our families and live our lives. We want nothing more."

Behind us from the balcony above the entrance, a host of choral voices unleashes the resounding strains of the *Messiah*. Pulses quicken, throats choke up, tears roll down cheeks, hearts open wide as hundreds of voices come together. The tenor of shopkeepers commingles with the soprano of school children and the rough baritone of steel workers to fill every crevice with their harmonic longing to be free. For over an hour the strident sounds reverberate with the bishop's message and pleas for patience and understanding.

Now, silence again. Almost two o'clock. The bishop prudently has left, realizing that time here is controlled. No one moves. We are riveted. We are stone. Fifteen minutes. Twenty. Thirty.

A stone shifts its weight. A hush of sound as more stones edge about. A few people file out.

Three o'clock. The cathedral is empty. I go outside where it's been snowing, leaving the city silent, muffled. An occasional figure scurries past, heading for the warm familiarity of home and family.

I gaze up at the St. Vitus spire, proudly silhouetted against the crescent moon broken by scudding clouds high above and wonder about all the tragedies it has witnessed. Nothing like what it is witnessing now.

Then it hits me. This is what freedom *really* means. Not the slavish search for material things, or the unbridled quest for fame—but the power to live a free and open life. *This* is what the people are fighting for. It will take a long time, yet I cannot but believe that in the end their quest will prevail.

The Russian winter will last twenty long years.

CARLA

Part 1

Los Angeles, CA, 1976

Sitting in the stuffy Burbank Social Security office, Kevin Almeida did his best to get across to Mr. and Mrs. Thornton that they were denied their claim for financial assistance because their personal assets "exceeded the allowable limit."

Their combined pension and Social Security payments were indeed low enough to qualify, but the house they owned, purchased in 1947 for $23,500 and now assessed in 1976 at over $200,000, was way more than the maximum allowed for physical property. Kevin commiserated with them but in the end could do nothing. The law was the law. They simply were too "wealthy." The only way to qualify was to sell the house they'd lived in for thirty years. Otherwise, the best he could offer was to encourage them to appeal the decision. He promised to write a strong recommendation for their case based on any new information.

The whole business sucked as far as he was concerned.

He stood up and walked the downcast couple to the door, damning the whole world. Why the hell did he ever take this job? Simple, he needed to save enough money for a year in Hong Kong to complete his PhD research. But was it worth it? As an SSA Claims Representative, he interviewed applicants for retirement benefits, financial assistance, or disability support. Not the most exciting job in town.

He picked up the next file, and called out, "Mrs. Rodriguez." A statuesque woman wearing a plain burgundy T-shirt and jeans stood and approached his desk. She appeared to be about his age, mid-thirties, with a head of shoulder-length wavy black hair that bounced and jounced the way the rest of her did. Despite her size and modest limp, she carried herself with ease and confidence as if dismissive of anyone who looked askance at her.

When she sat down, her mane of curls wreathed an oval face of dark eyes, and pouty lips giving her a come-hither look. This would not be an easy interview. He was determined to keep a balanced attitude and pay her no undue attention. Like focusing on his mashed potatoes while sitting next to Jayne Mansfield.

He had her take a seat on the other side of the desk and read over the claim form, glancing at her from time to time. She sat quiet, coy with a saucy expression. How could she be so provocative simply sitting in a chair in a Social Security office?

Carletta Gloria Rodriguez, born August 2, 1945, in the Midwest town of Grimes, Iowa. Education: GED high school certificate, plus two years of night classes at Los Angeles City College. Current employment: None. Work history: waitress, bar maid, domestic. Marital status: Divorced. One dependent child, a daughter, three years old. Mrs. Rodriguez was applying for a "recon," a reconsideration of being denied a claim for disability. In this case, she was filing a double claim: one for disability, and one for Supplemental Security Income (SSI), a less pejorative term for "welfare."

Kevin read over the three-page decision not to allow her the benefits. Two years previous, she'd been riding behind her boyfriend, Louis Gomez, on his motorcycle at the intersection of Sunset and Vermont in Hollywood. There was some dispute over who had the right of way, Louis or the guy whose Mercedes smacked into them. Whoever was at fault, she lost her left leg above the knee in the accident.

She made the simple argument that by being one-legged, she wasn't able to carry out her duties as a waitress or barkeep, her primary means of work. The Feds didn't buy it. After all, she did have a prosthesis, meaning she wasn't one-legged. Many people with artificial limbs were ninety, or even a hundred percent able to carry out "wait help" work. Ergo: denied, though the decision did allow for a six-month supplement for physical therapy.

Her current claim, the recon, stated that her condition had worsened. She tired quickly and easily, and she was unable to be on her feet for eight hours. Further, she alleged her mental faculties and ability to concentrate had deteriorated and she had fallen behind in her classes at Los Angeles City College.

Kevin shuffled the papers, had her sign the appropriate forms, and told her he'd write a recommendation to reconsider the decision, based on a doctor's confirmation. He had his own doubts, but his responsibility as a Social Security rep was to help the client as much as possible.

"All right, Mrs. Rodriguez—"

"It's Carla."

"Very well, Carla. I'll get on this, though it may take a while. I'll contact you as soon as I learn anything. In the meantime, I may need a further interview. I'll also have to examine your personal financial records."

She flashed her enticing smile. "I appreciate that, Mr. Almeida."

"Done. And it's Kevin."

The two-plus years he'd worked for Social Security had included interviews with plenty of attractive women whom he'd liked to have dated. The government, of course, was particularly strict about not fraternizing with clients and for obvious reasons: you lose your objectivity. Fortunately none of them had had enough appeal to pull him off balance.

Yet something was ticking already. Steering Carla to the exit door, Kevin glanced at her and felt the tug of attraction, not only *for* her but *from* her.

He thought of two magnets having opposite poles that draw on each other until you put them together and achieve a neutral forcefield, something he'd picked up in his high school Physics class. Such magnets can never have physical contact. They can come infinitesimally close but never quite touch. The idea intrigued him.

Driving home from work he thought about that. If there was anything to it, then that put paid to any relationship with Carla and that was probably a good thing. Stow it, Kevin, and do your job the way you're supposed to.

Except that wasn't enough to dispel his attraction to her. He more carefully reviewed her application. Uncertain of what he was looking for he dug into the report looking for details or any unusual information trying to get a "fix" on her. He sensed something different, something odd. Something without an ending.

He had to learn more, he had to see Carla.

A few days later, he decided to visit her for "further data." Maybe if he saw her away from the office, out of the world of officialdom, he'd find the answer and learn how cursory was his initial infatuation for her. And maybe help her with the application as well. He arranged to meet her at three.

She lived in a tiny one-bedroom apartment, part of a duplex, on Burbank Boulevard with her daughter, Dana. Based on her application, she paid $165 a month. From the outside, her place looked it, spare and seedy. Flower beds growing weeds. A beat-up seven-year-old Chevy Camaro, a "rust bucket," parked in front. The screen door hung from its top hinge, held open by a string attached to a stake in the ground. A French window missing a pane needed replacing. A worn "Welcome" mat lacked the "l".

Kevin didn't have a good feeling about this. Especially when he heard a kid screaming and, he guessed, Carla screaming back in a tooth-and-tong battle that shut down the instant he leaned on the doorbell button. Muffled sounds replaced the clamor. Carla opened the door, fussing with her hair. Standing barefooted, she wore shorts and a black halter which instantly drew his attention.

"Oh, Mister Almeida...hello." She turned to her watch. "My goodness, it's three o'clock already. Right on time, Johnny on the spot, aren't we? Please excuse the mess. Dana and I were..." She turned to look inside. "Our friend is here, Dana, would you like to say hi."

Kevin heard a weak "hi" from behind the door.

She nervously pulled a length of hair behind her ear.

"Mrs. Rodriguez...I mean Carla, this may be an inconvenient time. I can make another appointment, no problem."

She opened the door wider. "No, please, it's all right. I was having a...a little talk with Dana, but she's okay now. Please, do come in."

He followed her inside to find the interior equally shabby. The worn sofa sagged, a stuffed chair had gone to seed. A tattered carpet cried out for replacement. The kitchen sink was badly chipped, scuffed linoleum. A pair of mini refrigerators sat side-by-side, one whose door stood wide open. "On the blink," Carla explained. A child's things lay helter-skelter.

With a hint of embarrassment, Carla quickly apologized for the squalor that she and Dana shared and moved about picking up Dana's toys. Kevin passed on that, aware of how difficult single parenting must be.

With typical official suspicion, he wondered if her contrition wasn't preplanned. He knew how wily clients might be in order win a claim.

As soon as Kevin took his seat, Carla excused herself to the kitchen. "I don't have much, maybe iced tea?

"That sounds fine," though he really didn't care for tea, hot or cold.

Carla returned with a tall glass of something brownish brimming with ice cubes and a plate of Ritz crackers.

While nursing his tea, Carla proudly introduced her daughter, Dana, a pert little Shirley Temple, complete with the curly blonde ringlets. After a few minutes of playing small talk with Dana, Carla completed her impromptu clean up. She pointed to several sizable moving boxes from Allied Van Lines sitting in a corner crammed with papers.

"There you go, Kevin. My entire life is in those cartons. Help yourself." She paused. "You did say you'd have to examine my things, didn't you?"

He didn't relish the idea of going through all that, but at least it gave him an excuse to see her. Only two weeks after their initial interview, Kevin was transgressing the firm prohibition of agent-client fraternization. He knew it, and he knew Carla did too.

On the spot, he concocted a plan of sorts. "There are too many to do all at once. I'll take two at a time."

"Of course, do what you must."

Included among the papers, the majority of which were financial records, were her school transcripts. What intrigued him most were those of her four semesters at LA City College.

Kevin had never seen anything like it, as if someone had doctored her grades or made them up. In all the classes she'd taken, having just completed her fourth semester, she'd received nothing but an "A" grade. Not even one "B." A perfect 4.0 GPA. Nor had she skimped on the subject matter, none of the "basket weaving" courses many athletes took to keep them enrolled to collect their scholarships.

Carla met her curriculum head-on: English Lit, US History, Spanish, Psychology, Physics, Algebra, Calculus, Sociology. Even so, he was skeptical. Himself a college graduate and currently on leave from his doctoral program, he knew that grades were mere number-crunching that often camouflaged something less than peerfect. Twenty classes, straight A. Enough for two years on the Dean's List.

The icing on the cake came when he read professors' comments on applications for scholarships or membership in various organizations. Nothing but stellar.

"The brightest student ever in my twenty-seven years at LACC."

"Thorough and incisive in her analyses."

"Reaches beyond the required assignments."

"Diligent, insightful, original."

Kevin wasn't sure what to make of the accolades. He recalled how she claimed her attention span had deteriorated. He needed more of her background which meant he'd have to see more of Carla.

The following week, he made a second visit to return the two boxes, five more left. He didn't need to go but gave in to impulse. Besides simply wanting to see her, he justified the appointment by providing a new set of papers to complete for her SSI application.

As she often did, Carla toyed with her hair or tinkered with things, a letter opener or button on her blouse during their discussion. He noticed how she always needed to fiddle with something, to have an item in her hands. She liked to touch things.

"I've looked through your school records. Your achievements are outstanding. How did you manage a 4.0 with all those classes? You carried a pretty heavy load."

"I don't really know, Kevin. I love learning about new ideas, seeing something differently. I suppose I have a curious nature. I'm very nosy," she added, lightheartedly.

He demurred. "Your record is outstanding. But one thing I don't understand. You said you were falling behind in your classes. What classes?"

She answered from the kitchen where she was fixing a root beer float for them and Dana. "I guess I didn't have a chance to tell you, I just started at Cal State LA. It's something for people with special interests. I was lucky to qualify. It's too soon to post any grades, so no records."

"What kind of program is it?"

"Not really a program, an experimental curriculum put together by some of the faculty, 'Paranormal Psychology.' Some professors don't want it. But I convinced the Psych Department to let me work on my own with interested faculty. Kind of a self-study deal."

A couple of months after filing the reconsideration, an agent, Ken Barclay, from SSA's regional office phoned Kevin, thanked him for supporting Carla's recon, and said the agency had decided to allow the disability claim. Kevin felt good about that until he learned the reasoning. It stopped him dead in his tracks.

"Kevin, we're going to accept her claim, but it's not because of the amputation. This is in the strictest confidence, but you need to know this in order to carry out a thorough check of her finances though even then she may not be qualified."

"Go ahead."

"If her physical condition was the only problem, she'd still be able to function sufficiently with her prosthesis. Her records show she even won a dance contest at City College last year."

Kevin had learned that but only after he turned in his determination to support her. He'd let it stand.

"So what are these new circumstances?"

"Our new decision is based on her severe psychological problems. Preliminary tests reveal strong self-destructive tendencies. She may be open to suicidal, or even homicidal impulses, especially when under pressure. Any number of 'triggers' can set off seizures or spells. Alcohol or drugs can do it. So can a perceived menacing situation: a dark room, flashing lights, threatening sounds. That sort of thing. Until she's examined further, we won't know for sure, but she might very well be psychotic."

Homicidal or suicidal. Psychotic. "Oookay, what's the next step?"

"I'll contact the Psychiatric Division to schedule a more thorough interview. We'll send you a complete report of our findings. In the meantime, you'll have to confirm her financial status to qualify for SSI. Go back five years to any record you can access. Bank accounts, mortgage papers, alimony, child support, every source of income and assets no matter how trivial they may seem."

"Right, the standard procedure."

"More than that," Ken hesitated. "There's a reason why you need to look especially carefully into her finances. A preliminary investigation shows that as recently as two years ago, Mrs. Rodriguez may have had assets exceeding a million dollars."

Wham. "You sure about that? How does a person lose a million bucks in two years?"

"When you find the answer to that, you'll probably uncover her disability."

"I'll keep it in mind."

"Incidentally, the IRS has shown some interest in the case. Ditto, the DEA. Has Carla ever said anything, however oblique, about narcotics?"

"Not a word. You don't suppose—"

"Has she ever been to Mexico?"

"I have no idea. She was married to a guy from there. Something going on?"

"There's always something going on in Mexico. You might look into that, surreptitiously of course."

"Of course."

"Don't get involved in a lot of detail, we've got our guys working it. Just keep it in mind."

A million bucks. Two years. Mexico. Narcotics. He set out to delve into Carla's background and find the answers.

Social Security already had the basics. Born and raised in Grimes, Iowa, to Carl and Etta Simpson who named her after themselves. Carl plus Etta, hence Carletta with an "e", not Carlotta with an "o." That and her failed marriage to Carlos Rodriguez accounted for the Latino name. Kevin found no record of a divorce.

Carla's parents had eked out a meager existence. Father: occasional handyman and bookie. Shaky evidence of some drug activities. Mother: homemaker. In Grimes, Carla left home several times for weeks or months, possibly due to "sexual abuse" from the father. The "sexual abuse" comment was triple underlined.

At fifteen or sixteen, she left for good, made her way west and settled in Southern California. Addresses from police and juvenile detention files and police records trace her route: Topeka, Oklahoma City, Amarillo, Phoenix, Albuquerque, Blythe, CA, then on to Barstow and Riverside. The record revealed a five-year gap between Riverside and Los Angeles.

Was she in Mexico during that time? Pushing drugs? Kevin was getting carried away.

According to police and state unemployment archives, her first address after Riverside was in South Central LA, a tough, gang area. Within two years, her assets went straight up. Then fifteen months later, they crashed to ground zero on a roller coaster ride from bust to boom to bust. Like a starlet who comes from nowhere, makes the big time, and loses it all. That was Carla.

The chronology was sketchy, the details vague. She had worked as a "waitress," as she indicated on her claim forms. But there are waitresses, and there are waitresses. At some point, in her late twenties, she met up with another woman of similar means, name unknown, though referred to as "Gigi." At this point, the record goes dim.

Kevin knew he had to talk to Carla, try to get into her head as well as to examine her financial documents.

He continued to skirt the dividing line between necessary visits and extracurricular affairs. He'd become infatuated with her, always making sure he needed to verify some bit of information. He returned all the boxes and explained to Carla that he didn't want to keep them and preferred they remain in her apartment. He'd already looked them over and if he needed more detail he'd return to her place.

One night, after a few months of visits, they sat together in Carla's living room. As often happened, Dana was watched by Carla's parents who shared the duplex. They had returned from their first public foray together to dine at the Palomino nightclub in North Hollywood. A young Bruce Springsteen provided a wild night of music. Bruce had just begun to make waves with a best-selling album under his belt, "Born to Run."

Carla let her hair down after what Kevin believes was weeks if not months of self-imposed isolation from society. Lounging in her apartment, feeling satisfied after their night on the town, they made small talk until Kevin checked his watch. "Wow, nearly two o'clock, time's up."

She smiled and uncoiled herself from the sofa. Without a hint or a word she took his hand and led him to the bedroom. Again, the coy expression.

She always left the night light on. Some people prefer that, others want the dark. Kevin didn't care. Did Carla leave it on to emphasize her amputation.

"Ever seen anyone work a prosthesis?" she said, sitting on the bed.

"Never have."

"I'll show you." She opened her robe to reveal the leg. He tried to focus on the plastic-rubber-aluminum extension fitted firmly to the stub above where the knee had been and affixed with a leather strap to her upper thigh.

"It's easy." She deftly loosened the strap and removed her "leg" as easily and as quickly as a football player taking off his helmet. She did this looking at Kevin rather than the leg as if challenging him. "See, no problem," she said, but he heard the bite behind her indifferent pretense.

He made a studied look, noting how the surgeon had left some extra skin to wrap over the stub and cover the suture.

"Very neat," he said.

She concurred, obviously proud of the workmanship. But he didn't know if she was trying to impress him with the handiwork, or the fact of her loss? He wasn't sure how to react. Best to key on Carla's emotion *at the moment* since it swung wildly from time to time. He didn't know if she was schizophrenic, but there definitely were sudden mood swings.

A week later when he dropped by the atmosphere had changed. Despite the partial award—pending further investigation—SSA's probing into her finances had darkened her mood. Once, again, she hauled out the boxes stuffed with legal papers, contracts, bank books, receipts, check stubs, promissory notes. He spent the next week at work combing through them all, again.

She hadn't reached a million but wasn't far off. Based on what he found, the high point of her net worth occurred on July 23, 1975, shortly before she turned twenty-six, when her total assets topped out at $966,792. One year later, when she filed her recon, July 15, 1976, Carla's wealth, including pots and pans, her old Camaro, even the clothes she wore, amounted to $532.45. Documentation about where the money came from or where it went was spotty at best, certainly nothing that added up to a figure approaching a million. What the hell had happened? Did she have it stashed away somewhere?

He found himself caught in the middle. Does he go with her, or with the Agency? He struggled with the desire to allow her the maximum leeway, and at the same time to hold to his professional principles.

Which was getting harder to do. He'd known her barely six months and they had become a comfortable couple. Carla was tantalizing in whatever she wore. Even casual everyday clothes, her mere presence turned heads, men and women alike. Somehow she'd compensated for her missing leg by standing and walking erect with assurance. Her bodily movements demanded attention.

So when Carla received an invitation direct from Dean Meriwether not only to receive a special "Exceptional Achievement" award from the University president, but also to deliver the valedictorian address to the entire student body, she accepted, albeit with some hesitation. "I think I can do it, Kevin. I want to try. Will you support me?"

"Absolutely. I know you'll make it, Carla. I'm proud for you." he said, hiding feelings of guilt and apprehension. He hadn't been in public yet with her except for a few short trips to the store and the evening at the Palomino where the crowd was too drunk to care. Now he'd be openly escorting a woman whose application for government emolument he officially represented. Not only that, she and her escort were expected to dress semi-formally in front of a large audience. He tried to temper her excitement but knew her well enough by now to be ready for anything.

Plain yet fetching. She had put together an ensemble that she'd bought especially for the occasion, of black velour ankle-length culottes and a matching vest over a white long-sleeved silk blouse with peaked ruffles, leaving the top three buttons open until Kevin quietly buttoned up the third. "All in the name of professionalism," he told her.

Fetching, indeed. Her allure graced each move she made or position she held. The seductive audacity of which Carla was a master challenged even the most stoic observer. Kevin heard the audience gasp and murmur when she walked on stage.

As expected, the dean officiated the proceedings, including introducing her as valedictorian. Kevin sighed with relief and took himself out of the picture. The last thing he and Carla needed was to be seen as what they had become, a close-knit couple. He hadn't intended that, but those magnets.

And he truly was proud. At the post-commencement soiree, Kevin inwardly beamed at how many faculty and staff hovered near her, commending her with accolades and well wishes for a bright future. Kevin remained apart, not wanting to break the spell Carla must surely be enjoying and which she deserved. Just as important, he needed to remain anonymous and avoid being seen by a colleague.

Afterward, she presented Kevin with a photo of herself in exactly this outfit. She sits straight and confident, wearing black-and-white coordinates, her hands laced resting on one knee. Her torso faces forward, while her head is turned to the left looking past her shoulder. Her thick black hair frames an oval face. She dominates the picture not with her physical stature, although in a sitting pose it's obvious she is a large elegant woman.

Not even her eyes tell the whole story. They stare at the camera as if challenging it. Deep black pools. What really jumped out at Kevin was the mouth with its pixie smile-smirk. Carla's expression was the closest he'd ever seen to Da Vinci's enigmatic "Mona Lisa." The tantalizing moment reflects many things to many people. But Kevin had the advantage of knowing Carla personally. He pondered her persona. How little he knew about her aside from their liaison.

Then it dawned on him: it's the magnet. Close in until two opposing forces, or personalities, kept them apart. Meaning that her pixie Mona Lisa smile was not coquettish but represented a challenge, a dare, even confrontation cloaked in a compelling allure.

"Okay, in order to make your case, Carla, I need to know where your money came from. You understand that don't you?"

She pursed her lips, closed her eyes, waited a few seconds, then looked up and took a deep breath. "I met a girl, like me, same age, Gwendolyn—I called her Gigi, having a rough time of it. We hit it off, thought if we worked together, we'd do better. We did pretty well, you know." That impish smile again.

"Pretty well doing what?"

She jumped up, cradled her arms. "At Century City, working the conventions there. Always high-rollers wanting to meet a woman. I couldn't help it, Kevin. It was them, not me!" She stomped around the room, twisted on her prosthetic, anguished, turned to face him with a wild-eyed look. "Them!"

At that moment, he recalled the movie, "The Three Faces of Eve," about a woman with three distinct personalities. From his short time with Carla, he knew she could turn her moods on and off in an instant. How many personalities did she have?

He wanted to bolt. "Who, Carla? What do you mean?"

"Servicing men, Kevin. I was a *fucking whore*, okay?" Kevin noticed Dana in the corner, staring at her mother.

Carla ran her fingers through her hair, trying to gain stability. "Gigi and I did whatever it took to fleece those high-and-mighty bastards. They were ugly and evil, but they had loads of money."

Whoa, this was getting out of hand. "Hold on, Carla. Easy. We don't need to go on. It's okay. You want to take a walk, get some fresh air?"

She ignored Kevin, took up her glass, and gulped the rest of her drink down. She poured a third.

"No, I'll tell you exactly how I made all that money. A lot of it came from smart investing. I'm no dummy. But the seed money came out of hard *physical* work. After a couple of years here, in LA, I knew pretty much where the action was. Century City in Beverly Hills. Constant around-the-clock conferences and meetings of all the high rollers. Presidents of this, CEOs of that, chairmen of something. How they looked down on us, used us, ridiculed us. Tons of men, rich, powerful men." She paced back-and-forth reliving her sordid lifestyle.

"Gigi and I *each* rented an entire *suite*, at the Century Plaza Hotel, a large living room and a separate bedroom. Word got out, and before we knew it, guys were lining up to get laid. They'd sit around, drinking, laughing, waiting their turn. To be sure I'd make it with all of them, I'd take on two or three or more at a time, getting it every which way. Try to imagine taking on five guys at once, Kevin. On a really busy night, I didn't even stay in the bedroom, just took off my clothes and went around naked, letting them do whatever they wanted."

He wanted to stop her but she was in high gear on a down slope.

"Gigi and I started off charging twenty bucks a trick. Once we caught on, it went up from there. After six months, we were getting as much as a hundred, even a hundred-fifty a trick. Sometimes, even two hundred for doing really kinky stuff. And working twenty guys a night, each of us."

Kevin tried to calculate but his brain was racing. He looked up at her. "Give or take, that's three thousand…a night. Comes out to—"

"A hundred grand for a good month. Sure, we took days off, and sometimes nothing was going on. But in six months, I made nearly half a mil. Lived well, and still had plenty to invest. Real estate, mostly residential. At one time, I owned a dozen houses and I don't know how many apartments. Maybe a hundred. Stocks and bonds. In fact, at one time I had more than twice what you came up with. Closer to two mil."

"I need to check that out."

She shook her head. "A lot of it wasn't recorded. I had a couple of cool accountants, seduced them to cook the books. There's not much to check."

He stared at her, trying to grasp it all. "That's pretty hard to swallow. Two million dollars," wisped a smile.

"You think I made it up? That wouldn't make sense. I'm applying for government welfare, why raise the amount?"

"Didn't the police ever get involved?"

"Of course. I was in jail a few times for soliciting. But we jacked those guys who covered for us. We had them by the *cojones*. Squeal and we blow their cover. Play along and you'd get a freebie. But mostly we paid them all off. After all, guys are guys." He heard the rancor in her voice.

Kevin sat, dumbfounded. Two million bucks. For some reason, he didn't doubt her at all.

"Fair enough. What became of it all? How'd you get rid of it? Do you have any more stashed away?"

"I wish. That's the Cinderella story, only I never found my other shoe." She gave me a saucy look. "Pun intended."

She sat down, her hands clasped. "Once Gigi and I found our pot of gold we called it quits and went our own ways. For a year, I really lived high on the hog, queen of the ball and all that. Then I met Carlo. Carlo and Carla, get it? Kind of cool, don't you think?"

He remembered finding her marriage certificate to Carlos Rodriguez Obredo.

"I really took to him, thought he was so cool. He knew how to treat a woman, turned me into a queen. Just another guy using me but I didn't care. I realized then that they all used me. Everybody uses everybody. That's why I have to protect Dana."

"So you married Carlo. What then?"

"We had our wedding and reception on the Queen Mary, you know, the ocean liner anchored in Long Beach. Rented the whole ship. Set me back seventeen grand. Pocket change."

"You had the two million when you met Carlo? Did he know that?"

"Some of it. He knew I had a lot, but not that much. Then…" she paused. "He was always asking me for more, for investments he said. I said, what investments? Oh, some deals in Mexico. I'd been around enough to see through his so-called friends. He was dealing with narcs, mean guys, the kind that treat women bad, mis…something. Can't remember the word."

"Misogynist."

"That's it, misogynist. I decided to pull out. Fortunately, they didn't seem to care. I had them believing I was nothing but a used-up old whore. But they didn't know I had investments in the US."

Kevin held up his hand to slow her down. "You still have them?"

Carla shook her head. "As soon as Carlo found out he insisted I turn them over to him."

"Did you?"

"Only enough to keep him off my back. I delivered a stash of cash, mostly twenties, about a hundred grand."

Kevin raised his eyebrows. "Not bad for a day's work."

"He ran with some pretty bad hombres."

"That's a long way from two million which you say you no longer have. I need to verify that."

"I know, let me explain." She took a deep breath, calming her outburst. "Within a year, once I convinced Carlo that I was wiped out, we split. I went back to my old ways, going out with whoever I found, slipping back into the pattern of needing guys and hating them all at once. But for once it was at the high end, not in the gutter as before."

"You must have had some pretty wild parties."

"That and more. As soon as I formed a close relationship, I felt threatened. Shrinks call it 'codependency.' Not sure what that means, but my life became a jumble of rollercoasters and bumper cars. I craved attention yet was repelled by it."

Kevin nodded. The magnets.

That's when the accident happened. In the middle of a major intersection, a big Mercedes Benz 450 SEL—of which Carla had her own—slammed into her leg, smashing it from thigh to ankle.

"My whole life turned upside down, like part of me died with my leg. I can't really explain, but I felt guilty for losing it. I wanted to die but couldn't take my own life because of Dana. And Kevin, I really tried to be a good Christian. I realized God was punishing me for how I made all that money. Filthy money and it controlled me, and God was helping me see this. I understood once I got rid of it all, I'd return to a normal, or at least manageable life. Every dollar I gave away made me a little better, like buying my way back into God's good graces."

She paused and looked at him with a pleading expression that he found disturbing. Worse, he sensed a threatening drift about her.

"You do believe me, don't you, Kevin?"

He wasn't sure. He was in uncharted territory. He wanted to level with her, tell her exactly where he stood, but didn't know how she'd take even his slightest doubt in her veracity.

"All right, Carla, I'll be honest. All of what you've told me so far has been unlike anything I've ever known. It's a pretty big mouthful to chew on." He hesitated. "I'll put it this way, I'm not completely certain I believe all of what you've told me, but I *want* to believe you, to believe *in* you. Do you see?"

Her next words set him back. She reached out to grip his hand, squeezed, holding it in a firm grip.

"You know, Kevin, we can make a great team, you and me. After all this mess is taken care of. You and me and Dana."

He didn't like the drift of their discussion. "Team?"

She nodded. "Don't you see? With what I have left, and it's considerable, and with my contacts here and in Mexico, we can make a killing."

Stunned, he struggled to come to grips with this revelation. What the hell was she talking about?

"So you didn't get rid of all the money? You have any left?"

Carla smiled. "Silly boy, of course I don't. If I did, I wouldn't be here."

Kevin tried to follow her line of thinking and see where it led but she pitched too many curves. He nodded and pushed on. "I hate to bring this up, but I need to know what you did with the money, how you ended up with nothing."

"Simple Kevin, I threw it away. Dumped it on anyone, people I didn't even know. I'd go to a party, dressed in a lot of expensive jewelry, *expensive* jewelry, top names, Piaget, Tiffany's, Cartier. Women congratulated me on a necklace, a bracelet, a ring, I said 'Here, it's yours.' And I took it off and gave it to them. So many times I did that. After the surprise wore off, they all took it, no questions asked. I met a friend of a friend who told me about his lifelong desire to own a Maserati sport coupe, I don't remember the model. I happened to be driving one. Right then and there, I gave him the keys and signed the pink slip. I walked home. I don't know how many cars I gave away."

"Probably no records to show that."

"Except for some sales. Nothing on the give-aways."

Her story brought to mind some information he once came across in researching her case. In some people, a suicidal tendency is often preceded by disowning or denying what one has. That in some way, ownership, especially of tangible items, is construed as ugly or evil. The more you have, the worse a person you are. If that was a correct assessment, in Carla's case ridding herself of all her possessions may have staved off her committing suicide. Is that what she meant?

"What about all your real estate? You had a lot of property at one time."

"Most of it I sold for pennies on the dollar or gave to charity."

"How much of this is on the record?"

"Some is, some isn't. A lot of the money…simply disappeared."

Keven sat speechless.

Carla took a deep breath, let it out slowly. "Well, there's my story, take it or leave it."

"What happened to all those people you…befriended?"

"Oh, they're long gone. I never saw them again." She smiled wanly. "Like everyone else, they used me." Then, in an instant, a dark look clouded her face. "Don't use me, Kevin."

"Never, Carla. How could I do that?"

"The way the others did. They took from me what wasn't theirs. What belonged to God." Her expression turned menacing. "That's what they're trying to do now, they're trying to take Dana from me because I can't work. Because I'm *crazy*! But she's mine, they'll never get her." I saw her eyes tearing. "Never!"

It was the first he'd heard about that. "She is your biological child, right? I need to be sure of that."

"Damned right, but not Carlo's, not that bastard's."

"Then who is the father?"

She sat silent, wistful. "I don't know."

"No idea at all? Any way to find him? It might help."

"Oh, I have an idea. One of those Century City 'gentlemen.' Most never wore a condom. I tried to wash myself clean afterward, but you can't catch them all." She sat rigid, her lips frozen in a straight line, her gaze staring through him, seeing nothing.

"Carla—"

"Help me, Kevin."

That's when everything broke down between them. Kevin grew fearful of what this girl-woman might do.

He tried to backpedal their relationship, to gain distance from her, but she had dug in and refused to let go. At all times, day and night, he'd hear a knock on the door. There was Carla. If his door was unlocked, she barged in even if he was with friends. If secured, she hammered on it until he had to open up. Once she smashed the lock and broke in. If he was on a phone call, she'd make up stories demanding that the operator intercept the call, tagged him when he went out. The situation got out of hand. He was trapped, couldn't get away from her. She continued her pursuit and refused to let go. She was stalking him.

He had to get out, but first to level with her, to tell her he was leaving. The moment he said that her face became a mask of sheer venom. No more pixie smile, now distorted into an ugly grimace.

"You can't do that, Kevin. I won't let you. I'll go with you wherever you go. It will be such fun to travel, and it will benefit Dana."

"I can't afford it, Carla. I'll be on a student stipend, barely enough for myself. This isn't a spur-of-the-moment decision. That's why I worked with Social Security for a while, to save enough to go to Hong Kong and finish my research. It simply isn't possible. I'm sorry."

"Yes, you always said you wanted to go there. Take us with you, Kevin. I'll find you anyway."

He saw no other option but to bolt, or more accurately to sneak out of the country in stages. First, he vacated his Burbank apartment. Fortunately, he had a friend, Elly Benson, who lived in the tony neighborhood of Los Feliz, near Griffiths Park, a world away from offbeat Burbank, who told Kevin to stay with her as long as he needed. From there, once he had his ticket and visa in order, he'd move to a cheap hotel close to LA International. Even so, he remained apprehensive. Carla was right, she'd find him no matter what.

He had one more matter to take care of: he had to close the case on Carla. He submitted an exceptionally strong and, he thought, convincing argument. Without question Carletta Simpson Rodriguez was eligible for one hundred percent disability retroactive to her original application date. The agency accepted his determination. In the end, he advised her of the decision and without saying anything to her, he purchased a ticket on Pan American.

He moved out of his apartment to Los Feliz. He didn't want to take a chance that Carla might somehow stymie his travel plans. But she rode his mind, he was letting her down, big time. He wanted to call her but not on Elly's phone. With a pocketful full of change he found a pay phone at a nearby service station.

He was both relieved and depressed when no one answered. After calling three times with no luck, he gave up. He even gave some thought to cancelling his flight, but he couldn't do it. He was running away, and it was a horrible feeling.

Prior to his departure, Kevin hoped to give Carla a forwarding address, but he didn't have one. As soon as he arrived in Hong Kong and settled into a temporary accommodation at the YMCA, he sent her a note telling her where he was and how to reach him. He heard nothing for three months.

Then one day he received a note, not from Carla, but from her mother, along with a short article from the local Burbank newspaper. Carla had been murdered. Her whole torso slashed and gouged and shredded over thirty times with a butcher knife—an image of her body lacerated with deep cuts leaving only slices of skin and bloody clumps of meat nauseated him.

Three-year-old Dana had witnessed the entire attack.

Carla's mother also wrote that a few days after the murder, a man she thought was a Mexican, came to the duplex, said he was Dana's father and took Dana away. The Simpsons didn't know what to do. Their granddaughter stolen from them. By whom? She'd be four now. Where? US? Mexico? In the end, they did nothing and eventually moved back to Grimes, Iowa.

God knows what kind of trauma Dana must have experienced.

Kevin finished a year in Hong Kong, focusing on his research, while his memory of Carla's world dimmed, though it never disappeared. The magnets were working. Her persona had been compelling. He dwelt on their relationship, the good times and the bad. She was under his skin.

When he returned to the US, he wasn't surprised when he found himself checking the records section of the Burbank Police Department and City Hall. He was surprised to find nothing under Carla's maiden or married name, or variants thereof. Nor any information on Dana. Why was that?

What happened to the two million? She'd teased him that some of it still existed, stashed in a hideout somewhere. Without Carla herself, no way to find it.

The murderer? A drifter, sentenced to twenty-to-life.

Out of curiosity and for nostalgia's sake, he decided to check out her old place, the one on Burbank Boulevard. It hadn't changed. The same seedy rundown setting, only this time an old Ford pickup sat in the front yard resting on blocks. Nothing that hinted at its former occupants.

Kevin sat in front of the duplex apartment, half expecting Carla to appear, with Dana trailing behind her. He reached to open the glove compartment and extract a photocopy of the picture he'd long held safe. To protect it? To protect Carla? Every time he looked at it he felt an odd but comforting warmth followed by a wave of panic.

That damned expression, the perky lips that might mean anything. Was she taunting him? Pretending to care, making certain no one find out that she, Carla, would in the end prevail?

Then something else, something I'd missed before—the eyes. Using a magnifying glass he made a startling discovery because he knew without a doubt that Carla was not cross-eyed. Yet, her left eye stares directly at the camera but the other, the right one, has drifted to the right corner of her eye. She's looking two ways at once. Double crossing eyes? Double-crossing Carla?

Everything about her called for different interpretations. Who and what was she?

Driving away, he tried to sort out all his emotions. Why really had he come here knowing Carla, her parents, and Dana wouldn't be? A magnetic paradox? A push-pull scenario? She lashes out then pulls him back. Even in death, Carla still had a hold on him.

Carletta Susan Simpson Rodriguez, RIP, 1976.

INHERITANCE

Central China, 19th century

Wubao bustled about to make ready for her first visitor. She swept the hard-packed dirt floor, put a glass and pitcher of water on the wood crate beside her bed, and hung a clean frayed towel across the back of the rickety wicker chair. She arranged an incense stick before the cracked wooden statue of Guanyin, the Goddess of Mercy. Any more than that turned the room into a stuffy cage, besides she didn't have enough to buy a second one. The faint glow from a beeswax lamp illumining the room provided a hint of warmth from the blustery weather outside.

Gusts of wind whiffled the drape hanging in the doorless entry.

Wubao's hut sat at the far end of a dirt path, far enough to separate her from the rest of the village. The remote location next to a pig sty and her extra means of livelihood kept her isolated from the local denizens.

She lived in a hamlet tucked away in a rural area of middle China. The nearest town of any size lay several days away on foot, or one day by palanquin, except no one in Honghua could afford such a conveyance.

The locals called their settlement "Exploding Flower," named after the profusion of peonies that grew thick around the perimeter of the village, but not in Wubao's garden. Hers had dried up from lack of water—she had to shuffle half an hour each way to a small stream to fill two buckets for her personal use, never enough left over for the plants. She sighed when she peered through the hole in her greased paper window at the dead blooms, now whiplashed and scattered by the increasing gusts.

She had grown used to the isolation though it did not prevent her from getting plenty of attention—derisive and taunting—even turning the tones of her birth name's characters, the lilting Wŭbăo, "Five Treasures," in uplifting tones (ĕ) into a harsh Wùbào, "Filthy and Cruel" in sharp falling tones (è). She had long ago steeled herself against the ridicule, accepting her fate.

At first, it wasn't like that. She came from another village like Honghua—all villages in China were alike—a three days' walk away from where she was born.

Right after she experienced her first bloodletting, a much older man appeared in the village and claimed her as his bride, that is, his property. She didn't know about that. There was no ceremony, and no official made a pronouncement, and certainly no piece of paper since no one could read or write. The only paper involved were cash notes. Neither did her family provide a dowry. Poor people in the villages could not spare one.

She didn't know her age then. Only that Feng Lei—people called him "Lao Feng," Old Feng— transported her to Honghua in a wooden cart to live with him and thereby severing her from her own people. He promised her mother that he would take good care of her. Within weeks, Wubao's mother died leaving her on her own with her "husband."

For the first couple of winters, Lao Feng treated her well enough, meaning he provided food and a bed to sleep in, while she maintained their meager household. They had little contact together other than occasional hasty, and unsuccessful, efforts to conceive a child. Despite doing all the right things, including taking pills made from rhinoceros horn shavings or rubbing her privates with palm seed oil, nothing happened.

By the third snowfall, Old Feng took to treating her unkindly. She'd done her best to please him, but to no avail. Instead, he went carousing with his men friends. Gambling at mahjong, getting drunk on the local sorghum whisky, "white lightning," and hanging out with girls younger than Wubao herself at eighteen, all painted up to look pretty.

She knew the cause of her husband's bitterness. She failed to produce a son. Twice, she felt the little one inside her struggling to come out. Twice, it turned out to be a girl. Old Feng, upset and angry, grabbed the newborn, still slick from her mother's womb, strode off and returned emptyhanded.

When she promised to try again, and again, Old Feng laughed at her, accusing her of angering the gods.

More and more, he invited men over for a few drinks—and then some. When at times they made advances on Wubao, Old Feng turned a blind eye, for a minor fee, of course. He and his cohorts saw it as a satisfying conclusion to a night of partying.

As much as she hated it, she proved an amiable pet. Word spread, and before long, Old Feng's friends dropped by even when he was away. In time, the villagers, especially the womenfolk, gossiped behind their walls. At the same time, Old Feng's friends, or on occasion men she'd never seen before became constant visitors.

Now and then, Old Feng gave her a copper coin or two. Just enough to keep her from complaining. On the other hand, more and more often Old Feng drank too much and took it out on Wubao.

One afternoon, the local commissioner sent his agents to Honghua to demand tax payment in advance, a favorite government ploy, plus interest, in addition to what they paid now. She didn't understand anything about taxes and interest, but she saw how it affected Old Feng.

The next day, he got roaring drunk and said he was leaving her to find a better woman. He slapped her hard on both cheeks and railed at her: "You are a simple miserable creature who deserves nothing. Your loins produce only useless little girls." He shoved her hard against the wall, hard enough to leave her in pain for several weeks. "*Ni bu tsun-zai! Wo pao-chi ni!*" You do not exist. I deny you.

Holding her injured side, she watched him pack his belongings and all their meager savings, save for a single *tael* of currency which might last her one month. With that he stomped out, never to return.

Forced to fend for herself, Wubao accepted the most difficult and most menial tasks, those no one else lowered themselves to do. She chopped wood into kindling that she turned into charcoal briquettes. She washed the village laundry. She cleaned and scaled the fish that grew in the local pond. She whacked people's rugs, some two or three times longer than her height. And, beyond that she took on even more extra work by agreeing to clean out the communal toilets and gather the night soil for villagers' gardens.

Exhausting work, from sunup to sundown. Yet, she never complained, thankful for these meagre sources, just enough to provide for her simple meals.

Over time, the villagers called on her less and less often. They looked on Wubao as a different sort, certainly not one of them. Her swarthy complexion repelled those who prized lighter skin which included everybody. When she looked in the mirror, she saw darker shading, but since she never knew her father, she could not be sure. She tried to explain that the change came from the charcoal's ash, dust from cleaning the rugs, and the sun that darkened her skin from those taxing chores. even as the stench from her lack of bathing turned people away.

Her words fell on deaf ears as one household after another stopped calling on her. Truth be told, many villagers wanted her to leave, to move on, or at least the womenfolk did. But then, who would take up the menial tasks? The men for a while enjoyed her company to the chagrin of their wives or mistresses. Once Old Feng left, her source of clientele disappeared. Now she relied only on visits by temporary workers passing through, on their way from Somewhere to Somewhere Else, and very little of that.

This left her with few choices. In China's strong patriarchal culture, she did not enjoy the option of returning to her family, in fact a great loss of face for them. Once a girl married and left her birth family, her connection was cut off, and she belonged to her husband's people.

Except that Old Feng didn't have any people.

She had only one way left to make a meager living now that her other work had disappeared.

Wubao didn't know how long she had lived in Honghua after Old Feng spoke for her, only that she'd lived there several winters on her own. At least ten of them because she counted that many on her fingers. Other people reached a higher number—twenty—by adding their toes. Where her own should have been, she had mere stubs. She recalled a time when her feet looked like everyone else's, but the toes had rotted away from a disease people called "numbing wind," emitting a fetid odor and forcing her to totter whenever she moved about.

Wubao sighed as she once more surveyed her abode, resigned to another day of entertaining passersby. She wobbled about, whopped the doorway curtain sending motes of dust dancing into the air and whisked away by the biting wind. She placed a cotton coverlet over the straw mat on her *kang*, the brick bed warmed by a flue that extended underneath from a corner stove.

To heat the room, she had to be sparing since she had no coal, only wood chips. These would have to do, because she earned just enough for a fire to cook her daily fare, a handful of rice and greens and, when her luck held, a few bites of catfish.

In the frigid winter months, the lack of heat in her room turned many visitors away. That and her "foot disease" kept potential clients, aside from the lowliest, from seeing her.

As her feet continued to lose their shape, fewer and fewer men parted the curtain. The few who turned up were out-of-towners, wandering merchants or destitute farmers looking for work, who rarely bathed and never changed clothes.

This meant fewer coins to buy food. How could she entice more customers in?

She'd tried so many ways to please those who approached her, encouraging them to return. She pretended to enjoy even the most repulsive acts. She forced herself to stroke their hardness, or put the foul-tasting thing in her mouth, struggling to blank her mind to avoid being slapped or beaten. Her visitors took delight in abusing her, laughing when they pinched her tiny breasts and she writhed in pain. When she felt them gush inside her, she tried to hurry away to wash herself. This often brought another drubbing.

She dreamed of a day when her skin would be free of welts and cuts and bruises, and when she'd no longer be forced to endure their sweaty, filthy bodies on top of her.

The one bright spot in her life occurred whenever the itinerant faith healer, Ah Poh, visited her. In spite of Ah Poh's stern and gruff demeanor, Wubao had taken a liking to the worldly-wise crone with her lined face, sparse graying hair and leathery skin, the one person who treated her kindly.

Before long, she enjoyed a special bond with the old woman. She trusted Ah Poh.

Wubao had been feeling listless for a time and wondered why. She had eaten her usual meager rations, washed her privates as always, took care of herself as best she could. Still, she did not have her usual energy.

She asked Ah Poh about this.

The old woman understood diseases and how to treat them. She had traveled far and wide, visited other places, and learned a good deal. Ah Poh had heard of a mysterious new ailment that had proved lethal that no one knew how to cure. For a long time, they didn't even have a name for it.

It came to be called the "love sickness."

"Love sickness?" Wubao said. "Love and sickness cannot go together. I do not understand."

"It's body love, not heart love," Ah Poh said. "Whatever its name, you must have inherited it from some man."

This puzzled Wubao. "I have heard of inheriting money and valuable things, but inherit a disease? This love sickness is very new and strange."

Wubao exhibited the first symptoms of the illness: listlessness and fever. Ah Poh related stories about women who slept with many men and who became tired and achy.

"That's why I have it?" she asked.

"Yes, it seems so," Ah Poh said.

But Wubao didn't know any other way to make a living except to sleep with men. Cutting wood brought in too little to live on, besides she no longer had the strength for heavy work like carrying logs or towing a wagon full of bamboo. Forget the laundry and the fish—the villagers did not want her touching their things.

Over the next few days, she regained enough strength to see her visitors. But after a while, she again lost her stamina, her stomach felt on fire, and a riveting headache made her nauseated. She called for Ah Poh, the one person she knew who could cure her, to fix her an herbal potion. Her mixtures always made Wubao feel better, and she eagerly consumed the drink.

This time, Ah Poh's treatment didn't help. Wubao managed to struggle through several more days, sweating from the excruciating spasm which reached into her groin. Then, after her final visitor wiped himself clean, she collapsed, too exhausted even to sup her gruel. The next morning, when Ah Poh came into Wubao's hut, she found her on the *kang*, whimpering in pain.

Coiled up, she grabbed Ah Poh's arm, clinging to the old woman, as if her touch had magic.

"Ah Poh, tomorrow is the Day of the Moon. I may have some visitors. Can you make me well again?"

Ah Poh had her lie down. She peered into Wubao's eyes, examined her tongue and saliva, poked and pinched and kneaded. Even sifted through her feces.

"I cannot be sure," the old crone said, "but you must have the love sickness."

"And I received it from the men?"

"Yes, and whoever sleeps with you will, in turn, inherit it."

"You mean I can give this to many men?"

"That's right," Ah Poh answered. "Anyone who sleeps with you can inherit it. Within a few months or even weeks, they will all get sick and die. No one knows how to stop it."

"Then after that, I am okay?"

"No, you cannot get rid of it even after passing it on to someone else. In time, you will die, just as they will die." Ah Po looked at her with a stern expression. "Once a man inherits the disease, not only will he die, if he sleeps with other women, they will die too."

Wubao felt a wave of anxiety race through her body. Her face drained of color. She sat on the *kang* and looked up at the old woman. "You mean I can cause many deaths?"

"Very many. Whoever inherits the love disease from you will meet their ancestors. None can escape it."

The immensity of this potential was not lost on her. "All of Honghua will die?"

Ah Po thought long and hard. "If my information is correct, then yes, the entire village could meet its end."

Wubao remained silent for a long time contemplating what Ah Poh had told her about passing on the illness. She thought deeply on this. If she already had the sickness, she'd for certain pass it on to her guests, and they on to others.

This gave her a strange feeling of satisfaction.

"Thank you, Ah Poh, for explaining everything to me," she said with a slight smile. "I must prepare myself for today."

Ah Poh looked at her with a puzzled expression, then parted the drape to leave. She stopped and turned. "Pray to your ancestors. Only they can help."

Wubao stood quiet. She knew of no ancestors. She had only herself.

And the power to transmit her inheritance.

IN THE FIELD OF A BLIND GOD

Burma (Myanmar), 2017

The acrid stench of something burning woke Shora from her afternoon doze. She rolled over and smiled at Nurul, eyes wide, staring at her. Whenever he first saw her, he pursed his lips and reached out to her to nurse.

Not this time.

She detected the movement of people stirring.

Before she could prop Nurul to her nipple, her mother rushed into the hut.

"Quick, Shora. We must leave. Get your things."

"Mama, what is it? I haven't fed Nurul yet."

"No time for that. Get a move on. Hurry."

Fully awake now, Shora heard popping sounds and explosions.

She pulled Nurul from her breast and put him down eliciting a full-throated howl.

She jumped up and hurried about the hut, taking a few items of Nurul's clothing. She grabbed her other *loungyi* sarong and a pair of *eingyi* blouses, and some plastic slippers.

She hastily laid a sheet on the floor, threw everything onto it, yanked the four corners together, and tied it into a small bundle. Then grabbed a towel and wrapped it into a *gaungbu* that she placed on her head to help balance the bundle and free up her hands. Picking up Nurul, she scrambled outside.

The popping grew louder, the smell stronger. The smoke made her tear up. She took a kerchief from inside her blouse and wrapped it around Nurul's head.

Her village of Khiladong in southwest Burma had erupted in chaos. People ran about shouting and screaming. She knew their fate if caught, just as she knew her own, a fresh sixteen-year-old nubile girl.

Frantic, hugging Nurul ever tighter, she found some of her family. Her parents, her sister Azara, and her grandmama Dahi. "Where are Yasin and Rashida?" she asked about her brother and husband.

"Over there," Azara pointed to a group of men trying to bring order to the families who lived in the village. She recognized some members, women and older men, and noticed others already trudging along the dusty road toward the river, away from the village, and the enemy.

Mama shuffled closer, her hunched back preventing her from walking straight. "Shora, take Nurul. Go with Azara and stay with the others. To the place where you fill the water buckets. We'll catch you up."

"After that, mama, what then?" she asked, reluctant to separate from her family.

"Just away from them," Mama said.

Shora tightened her grip on Nurul and adjusted the bundle on her head. She set out, fearing for the menfolk.

Shora caught up with the first group—a couple of dozen women and girls. They approached the next village, a twenty-minute hike beyond their own, where her husband, Rashida, came from. She knew some of the girls, but when they saw each other no one spoke. Their fear of the Tatmadaw—the Burmese Army—left no energy for conversation, fearful of doing anything to catch a soldier's eye.

They concentrated on keeping up with another group from a different village.

Soon, Shora and Nurul blended in with a scattered throng of hundreds, most carrying only what they wore. A few toted small bundles attached to ends of bamboo sticks jouncing on their shoulders. Or others, like Shora, a wrap of woven cotton on their heads. Women dressed in sarongs or ankle-length manteaux and hijabs. Men in pants and shorts and baseball caps or white *taqiyah* skullcaps. Many in T-shirts embellished with names or logos that none understood, like I♥NY. Most wore plastic flipflops or went barefoot.

Everyone shabby and filthy and weary and beaten down. And terrified.

The searing heat and humidity created a haze, that caused her skin to prickle and the usually quiet Nurul to grow fretful. She wanted to nurse him, but for now she could satisfy him only with a water bottle.

They continued to push on, passing yet another village, by now only a handful of deserted hovels.

She heard shouting behind her and turned to see a gaggle of uniforms, some waving torches, others brandishing machetes, most firing rifles or pistols, surround the village to make sure no human or animal escaped.

Amid the chaos of men shouting and women screaming, she searched in desperation for her family. Where were her parents, siblings, husband?

There, her Dahi grandmama, too weak to walk on her own, supported by Azara. Shora scrambled trying to reach them.

From the seething horde, Baba appeared, urging them to keep going. "Hurry," he yelled, helping anyone who lagged behind.

They were running for their lives. For one reason—they were Rohingya.

The rampaging troops drew near. Heavily armed with bandoliers of cartridges crisscrossing their chests. They wore dark khaki camouflaged uniforms, black boots, and large canvas field hats. All so young, many her age.

She watched them approach. When they reached the village, they fired wildly, spraying the area with bullets.

She saw bodies drop to the ground like sacks of rice.

Nurul screamed and screamed some more.

She glimpsed a dark sweaty face race past and saw hatred in the squinty eyes.

Shora's group reached another village, already abandoned, the fourth since leaving their own half an hour before. More yelling as soldiers with their torches moved through the village like seething ants, igniting everything, slaughtering the few remaining livestock. As each hovel in the village caught fire, a whooshing sound marked yet another thatched hut gone up in flames.

She recoiled from the pandemonium of pillaging troops and the frenetic cries of villagers. She wanted to cover her ears, to escape the turmoil around her.

The ragtag villagers slowed their trek.

What's wrong, Baba?"

"Soldiers have destroyed the bridge," he said. "Impossible to cross the river now."

She reinforced her grip on Nurul. "What do we do?"

Her father took her by the shoulders. She felt his fingers squeeze her and watched his mouth working to say something.

"Shora," he said with a desperate look, still holding her and Nurul and embracing them both. "Shora," he choked up, "I love you."

"I love you, too, Baba…and so does Nurul."

Her baba nodded. "I must leave now to help the older ones. You and Nurul, run, run for your lives."

And he was gone.

Tatmadaw teams spread out, converging on her group, punching, kicking anyone on the ground. Some villagers tried to help the weaker to stand only to be pistol-whipped or bashed with rifle butts.

She tasted the bile that crept into her throat.

Allah, please let us go. We mean them no harm.

Several soldiers surrounded the group, yanked the men aside. Women clung to husbands and fathers until the soldiers wrenched them away. They removed all males over the age of six or seven and bludgeoned anyone who resisted.

A frail wispy-haired man, too weak to keep up, tripped and fell to his knees. A hysterical woman broke away from the group. Before she could reach him, two soldiers grabbed her. She shrieked when they yanked and dislocated her arm. The old man struggled to crawl through the dirt to his wife. A soldier approached the prone figure, pushed his rifle barrel to the back of the man's head. Amid a convulsion of screams Shora heard the gun fire.

The other women, numb from shock, watched their menfolk pushed and prodded out of sight beyond the burning hamlet. Shora saw Rashid stop to look back at her before a Tatmadaw drove his rifle barrel into his back.

She buried her face into Nurul's belly, sobbing. She moved next to her Mama for mutual comfort, aching for her baba, her husband, her brother, her family.

Please, Allah, she prayed again, help them. Help us all.

The women congregated, whimpering, seeking solace among themselves.

In spite of being terrified, her adrenalin soaring, Shora grew weary, longed to lie down, but whenever a woman dropped even to kneel, a soldier yanked her up. The Tatmadaw made it clear they would beat anyone who moved about or made a sound. And they must stand upright.

The crackle of huts on fire and squeals of the few remaining animals the only sounds now. The burning villages stretched along their route seemed to spook the boyish recruits. She watched them as, wild-eyed, they shouted at the women.

Nurul knew only one thing—he was hungry. He wailed, water no longer sufficient. If only she could breast-feed him, but she was afraid to move, to do anything that might draw attention. Certainly not to loosen her *eingyi*. She stood helpless to quieten him. She slipped behind a bevy of women, who formed a circle to hide her and the squalling infant.

Embracing Nurul, Shora focused on calming him, and failed to notice anything until she heard a woman gasp. She saw the guards returning by themselves, without the men and boys. Her brain froze when she saw several of them wipe their machetes clean on banana leaves.

The women cried out, some slumped to the ground, weeping, sobbing. Shora left her hiding place to help Azara with Mama who stood limp.

"Mama, please. We are here for you. Don't leave us, Mama," she pleaded.

Her sister stood, too stunned to speak. No reaction from Mama, either. Only vacant eyes, until she closed them, murmuring prayers to Allah.

Dahi slumped to her knees, moaning.

Shora still did not register the impact of losing her father, brother, husband. She knew, but she did not feel.

Only emptiness.

The crying, the sobbing, the wailing of the women grew in volume.

It unnerved the soldiers. They went about smacking and punching the women.

She wanted to flee, to take Dahi and Mama and Azara and Nurul and run, like Baba said. Get away from this rapacious evil that had descended on them.

Because they were Rohingya.

She continued to hug, coddle, and hum to Nurul since she could not nurse him. He continued to cry until a soldier, his face bright with perspiration stood before her, barking an order in Burmese which she did not understand. Angered, he began shouting and slapping her.

She hugged Nurul, bowed, and offered apologies, and recoiled at his expression of total revulsion.

She tried to dodge his fist, felt the jarring blow to the side of her head. Stunned, she pleaded with him to stop.

Out of control, he yelled at her, pointed to Nurul, and pantomimed that she hand him over.

A cold rush of adrenaline streamed through her. She shook her head and clung to Nurul even tighter.

"No, never. Kill me, but don't touch my baby." She yelled a plea incomprehensible to the soldier. "PLEASE."

In a blink—quicker than her dulled senses could react—the soldier whipped out his knife and in one quick motion slashed her cheek. Too stunned to respond, she stood dazed and reached up with her free hand, then drew it back, laced with blood.

In that single moment, she also loosened her hold on Nurul. The man reached for her son, tore him away.

Shora let out a hideous scream and lunged at the soldier. Strong hands pulled her back.

Horrified, she watched the trooper hold tiny Nurul by one leg and fling him into a searing hovel, fully aflame.

Screeching and clawing like a caged animal, she grappled to break free. She fought with maniacal fury to save her baby, then stared in horror at the writhing lump of blackened flesh.

Hysterical, shrieking until reduced to a yammering, crazed animal-like being.

She lost focus, reduced to mumbling and spitting drops of foamy saliva and vomit.

"My baby, my son..." she cried and blubbered and gagged.

The same soldier, unable to deal with her, gripped his rifle, stood over the now smoldering mass of Nurul, raised the weapon, and drove his bayonet into the blackened corpse. Then, he raised it high, and shook it in front of her face.

Nurul—a charred lump.

The searing pang that exploded in her brain sucked her sanity. Her mind went blank, her senses shut down.

She threw back her head, emitted a single long screech, then another and another and another and another that crescendoed into a shrill animal cry.

Soldiers surrounded her. One clamped a hand over her mouth. He howled when she bit him and drew blood, the instinct of a feral creature.

She fought every way a sixteen-year-old girl could—kicking and biting and punching and scratching. They grabbed the front of her blouse and ripped it off. Then her sarong and her underthings until she stood before them naked. They threw her to the ground where two men planted boots on each arm to pin her down. Two others grabbed her ankles and spread her legs.

She heaved to break free, fell back when a pistol barrel smacked her across the temple.

The first soldier penetrated her. Then only when the men were satisfied did they finish.

She lay with eyes closed, her mind unaware of her surroundings until she felt the sting in her cheek and the pain between her legs.

Moments later, she felt heavy warm drops from an early spring rain splash on her face and body. As quickly as it started, the rain stopped.

Not rain.

She watched the men zip up their fatigues.

Finished, they grabbed their rifles, picked up machetes, and walked off, joking and laughing, fading off to the next village.

She lay supine, exhausted, her mind blank, unaware of her surroundings. Time had disappeared. Only when fading sunlight brought on evening shadows, and the shouting and screaming and pips of rifle fire died out did Shora stir. She blinked, but registered nothing, not even the lingering wisps of smoke and odors of scorched wood and flesh.

She rolled over and stood up, disoriented, bumbling about, haphazardly gathering a few things that lay scattered. She threw on a few scraps of her clothing hoping mama would approve.

She straggled toward the river, stumbled along a dusty lane, oblivious to the humps of rotting bodies.

Peaceful now. She hummed a little ditty her father had taught her.

Soon she would be with her family, praying to Allah with her papa and mama and Rashida, and cuddling chubby little Nurul.

She smiled.

REIKO MURATA

Tokyo, 1947

Reiko Murata knelt on the tatami mat in front of her polished rosewood writing table, studying the arrangement before her like someone contemplating a chess move. She sat back on her heels to make sure her calligraphy materials were in order: a sheet of rice paper, a brush, an ink stick and ink stone, a ceramic paperweight, and a pair of tweezers. Satisfied they were laid out in proper order, she placed an envelope alongside the brush.

She remained immobile, eyes closed, deep in thought, her mind absorbed by the breeze rustling through a stand of bamboo in the outer garden. Without seeing, without hearing, she felt her surroundings comfort her, like a protective barrier from the elements, from the outside world, enhanced by the musky trace of the lone incense stick.

Reiko wore a pure white kimono, the traditional color that represented death, and she had swept up her waist-length hair in the bouffant style of traditional courtesans. Not that she was one, it was simply her habit.

After some moments, she looked up.

As she had innumerable times, Reiko picked up the envelope on the table, opened the flap, and with the tweezers extracted the single sheet inside. She took her time to unfold the glossy paper, making sure not to crinkle its embossed edges. She spread it out on the desk in front of her, noted yet again its exquisite insignia indicating the Chief of Staff of the Japanese Imperial Navy. Its words had become seared into her memory from countless readings. Rather than perusing the note, she instead imagined its author sitting very like she was now, his brush sweeping across the page in bold powerful strokes.

My Dearest Reiko-san,

You know the situation facing our illustrious nation. Our revered Emperor has taken the unprecedented step of calling on us to lay down our arms. For a warrior who has vowed to fight the enemy unto death, this is a difficult order to follow. However, I must obey our august ruler, His Majesty, Tenno.

Reiko-san, by the time you read this letter, my spirit will be in Heaven, in Tengoku. Having served my country and my Emperor, I neglected my family. Our son died in a valiant endeavor, our daughter perished helping others. I failed to save them. You alone must endure the agony of survival.

Forgive me,
Taki

Reiko shut her eyes, softly, listening to the orioles chirping outside, recalling the first time she and Taki had visited Tokyo's Rikugi Park, noted for its landscapes, and its plethora of songbirds. How could any human write music to match such euphonious calls?

She opened her eyes and read the concluding *haiku*:

Blossoms have fallen.
All is finished.
Remember *shinpu*.

Shinpu = *Kamikaze*. Euphemisms for suicide.

The missive was dated August 16, 1945. In the months since then, she had received bits and pieces of information—some from official letters, others by word-of-mouth— regarding the death of Admiral Takijirō Saito. How he had committed *hara-kiri*: belly-cutting. She was not surprised, realizing ever since she and Taki married that he would make the ultimate sacrifice if necessary. She had also anticipated her Taki-san choosing the most excruciating option, the *jumonji*, the cross-cut, tracing the shape of the written character for heart, *kokoro*, across his abdomen. And he had declined a *kaishakunin*, a second, who decapitates the victim when the pain becomes intolerable.

He took fifteen hours to die.

Remember *shinpu*! What did her Taki-san mean by that? Had he meant for her to take her life? What about the line of his note counseling her to "endure the agony of survival"? Did he intend for her to continue to live and carry on the Japanese spirit? This was a mixed message. How could she "*shinpu*" and still survive? Her own death would change nothing.

Shimatta! Damn it! Reiko knew she was playing out the age-old dilemma of having to choose between *giri* and *ninjo*: duty and desire. Her duty was to her Emperor, her husband, and her family, in that order. But she also felt a duty to herself, which went way beyond the bounds of Japanese behavior. Her personal desire was to live, to *cling* to life. She enjoyed being alive, and the sensations of touch and taste and smell, and loving. Oh, damn tradition and obligation and slicing open your belly so your guts spill all over the place.

What was she thinking! And her children? Where were they now? Both dead. What would they think? Would they have wanted her to take her life?

Before he died, Taki wrote her that Makoto had led one of the first waves of *kamikaze* pilots against the American ships, and died "gloriously." She grimaced and envisioned him blown to bits in a burst of red billowing flames and twisted metal. Then Akemi, lighthearted and quick to smile, following her sense of *giri*, had left home to work for the Self-Defense Corps. She was incinerated in the ten-thousand-degree flash that obliterated central Hiroshima.

Reiko folded the well-worn note and inserted it into the envelope which she placed in a nearby desk drawer.

She looked up to view the pair of pine trees that grew majestically outside her windows.

They stood so straight and tall, yet pliant. She wished she was like that. If only she were a pine whose flexibility tempers and increases its strength to remain firm and resilient. But she was a mere mortal, a woman, a lowly human being, bound by tradition.

Even so, Reiko's mother had instilled in her a sense of independence: go with your heart. Honor those in your life without relinquishing belief in yourself. By failing to conform to Japan's inflexible customs, to defy her husband's intimation for her to *jigai*, to carry out her female suicide, she knew was bordering on blasphemy. It required her to resist one of Japan's most sacred edicts.

Her father would never condone such thoughts. A good man but bound to Japanese tradition by a strong sense of order: emperor, shogun, father, husband. He'd had no use for any female role except to help him support those figures. But Reiko's father had died in a local influenza epidemic when she was fourteen. In her formative years, she had learned from her mother that as strongly patriarchal as Japanese culture remained, women, too, had their place. Reiko came away with a strong sense of a woman's potential contribution to society.

Now, reading the haiku reminded her of the last time she had seen her husband alive. It was two years ago this month, May, 1945. American aircraft were leveling population centers daily. Japanese cities, built ninety percent of wood, turned into raging conflagrations in minutes, creating whiplash firestorms. In spite of official proclamations, everyone knew that Japan was losing the war. Taki decided to move his family to a house in an outer suburb of Tokyo to avoid the ever-increasing Allied bombing runs, and to protect his wife and children from atrocities that Japan's military government insisted the Americans would certainly inflict.

They had knelt before two enclosures, a shrine for honoring Buddhist deities, and an altar intended for Shinto gods. Reiko had watched her husband, incense clasped in his cupped hands, his forehead touching the *tatami*. He was not a handsome man. His craggy features, broad nose, and large ears reminded her of a caricature in a children's fairytale book. He was rather short, equal to Reiko, who was tall for a Japanese woman. He spoke the clipped Tokyo speech, when he spoke at all, and his habit of staring at his interlocutor could be off-putting. But underneath his rough exterior, Reiko knew, was a kind and compassionate man.

She had once listened to Taki explain his intent to remain with his unit until the end, whenever and wherever that was.

"Reiko-san, I must tell you, in the case of defeat, I cannot bear the thought of living even one day. I owe it to my Emperor, and I owe it to my men. I'm sure you understand."

She bowed her head and paused before answering, "Of course. I have known this from the moment I met you."

"As for you and the children…I leave it to you."

Reiko looked up sharply. "My husband, please guide me in this crucial decision."

Taki held up his hand. "When the time comes, you will know what to do…"

When the time comes.

That time will never come, she thought.

She drew from the drawer a scorched family photograph taken the day Taki left the last time for the front, the same photo returned with his personal effects, including an urn with his ashes. How proud her husband and children seemed, yet she wondered if they felt the same dread and anguish she did. Taki certainly did not, that she knew. Maybe their twenty-five-year-old son, Makoto, like his father, felt no fear. But she doubted it. He was also *her* son, even if he bore his stoicism well. Akemi, three years younger, was also close to Taki, but not to the point that she hid her feelings. She, like her mother, hated the war, and made no attempt to camouflage her displeasure.

Reiko's attention returned to the moment when she realized she'd tensed up and risen a fraction from her kneeling position. She took a deep breath to relax and sat back on her heels, pointing her toes inward, the way Japanese women knelt.

Remember *shinpu*. She was supposed to be ready to die by virtue of being the wife of a military officer. Japan's samurai culture expected the wife of an admiral to follow the Code of Bushidō, the Way of the Warrior. But her Buddhist upbringing, which did not condone suicide, told her not to.

Taki, give me an answer.

These thoughts had swirled through her mind for so long they no longer bore immediacy. She wondered if she had been forcing herself to dwell on them out of respect for her husband, rather than seeking a true solution. She needed answers but had no idea where to look. In the meantime, she would continue as before.

She put her mind to the task at hand, following the same procedure she performed every Friday afternoon at precisely 4:15, the day and hour of her husband's suicide. She once again prepared for her simple observance by picking up the ink stick and rubbing it on the stone, watching the water in the shallow well darken, as if a black cloud had permeated it. She took up her brush, dipped it in the ink, then elevated her elbow above the table, holding the brush vertically. With a steady hand, she wrote the same note she'd penned dozens of times.

Dear Taki-san,

Although I cannot reach out and feel you, I know you are here beside me. We cannot touch, we cannot embrace, yet your presence in my mind is more real than our transient lives.

You and I will live forever. Our spirits and our children's spirits shall never perish.

Your loving wife, Reiko

She looked over her handiwork. Her calligraphy was passable, people said, but the words had become banal after so many repetitions.

Reiko gave a sigh and stood from her kneeling position. Following her usual practice, she took the letter she had written to Taki-san outside to the *hibachi*, stirred its coals, and inserted the paper into the brazier. She watched it flare up in an act of ritual leave-taking.

If only her own confusion could so easily be erased.

A DEATH ON THE YANGTZE

Part 1

Yangtze River, Central China, 1985

The boat shuddered under a hard port turn, bringing the *S.S. Bashan* around one hundred-eighty degrees. The sharp change in course allowed Captain Wu to move into position and dock at berth 41, on the lower reaches of the Yangtze River at Nanjing.

I felt the helmsman yank the "Back Full" throttle and watched as the *Bashan* sidled into its slip. Able seamen on board stood by ready to toss hawsers to dock men who would loop them around bollards. That done, the engines idled then shut down.

A new tour group, sixty-two in all, mingled at the bottom of the gangplank, then single filed up. The usual array of Americans and a few Canadians. Some were no doubt very rich, though most of middle class. None were poor. I tried to gauge each passenger.

One couple stood out.

Jedidiah and Edith Boley might have stepped out of a one-room log-and-pitch hut from Little House on the Prairie. Jedidiah was tall and gaunt and weather-beaten with a thin gray beard and a sparse head of white straggly hair. He wore the raiment of the range—a sheep man with a long-sleeved red flannel shirt buttoned at the collar, and Rough Rider denim jeans, hitched up by a set of J-Clip suspenders. His shoes? Jefferson high-top brogans.

The only item missing from Mrs. Boley's attire—an ankle-length gingham dress ruffled at the neck and elbows—and laced-up shoes, was a hooded sunbonnet. Even without it, she brought to mind Ma Kettle. Mrs. Boley wore a tired smile, and walked with tiny, minced steps, struggling to keep up with her long-legged husband.

The provincial-looking pair reminded me of carpetbaggers, but their *Bashan* suite came in at ninety dollars *per person*, *per day*, more than any of the crew earned in a month, a goodly amount in 1985.

The Boleys made their way up the ramp, she holding his elbow, he grasping the handrail. Reaching the top, he roughly brushed aside helping hands from the *Bashan* crew. Edith, clearly embarrassed at the effrontery, apologized and waited patiently with her obstreperous spouse for someone to show them to their accommodations. Jedidiah coughed and grumbled as he ascended the stairway to their top-level suite of which the Bashan had only six.

I watched the vexed man and his meek and subservient missus climb their way to the second deck, Mrs. Boley guiding him as if caring for a recalcitrant patient. I felt sorry for her and took an instant dislike to The Curmudgeon. They disappeared into the passageway. I was curious how the Boleys would fit in with the others.

The *Bashan* qualified as a "ship" by virtue of carrying several smaller craft, dinghies for emergencies. In my thinking, only ocean-going vessels could be considered real ships. Since the *Bashan* limited its sailing to the Yangtze River and its tributaries, I figured it a boat.

A pretty nice boat, though. Management at the China Merchant Steam Navigation Company had spared no expense to assure the most comfortable accommodations, including hiring one hundred-twenty crew members to serve sixty-six passengers, a two-to-one ratio that would quickly bankrupt the most solvent capitalist shipping enterprise in Europe or America.

The four-deck, 260-foot craft had been converted from Mao Zedong's private yacht, *The East Is Red*. Mao, having died seven years earlier, no longer needed it. Designed to satisfy the most discerning guest, it was blessed with all the latest upgrades. Its forty-foot pool, bar, dance floor, salon, and viewing room filled with videos, was light-years removed from anything in China at the time.

I was one of four foreigners working for Lindblad, the upscale tour company that was the first to charter a Yangtze River cruise ship. Bill, a British chap born and raised in Kenya, was cruise director. Rounding out our quartet were Amy, our Swedish hostess, John from New Orleans, a piano bar singer and player, and me, a Sinologist, that is, a China "expert." I had it easy, giving half a dozen lectures on each weekly cruise and interpreting for the passengers. The pay was good: $US 100 per day tax free, plus generous tips, a private en suite cabin, all meals, and a free bar.

We plied the Yangtze from Chongqing, the Bashan's home port, to Nanjing, 800 miles downstream, once a fortnight, one week down and a week return—or more correctly, east and west— stopping at various sites along the way, with guided tours on shore. After two years, I knew pretty much about all the historical points of interest and had become old friends with locals onshore.

After assuring that all passengers were aboard and accounted for, we cast off from the Nanjing dock at six that evening for our return upriver. Most passengers nosed around the vessel until dinner, then repaired to their rooms, exhausted from having traveled for ten days at a grueling China tourist pace. Invariably, the *Bashan* provided a respite from travelers constantly on the move.

I noted that the Mr. and Mrs. Boley did not show for dinner, nor did I see them anywhere on deck.

The next full day we steamed west toward Yichang and the newly completed Gezhouba dam, and its locks. Raising and lowering a ship inside a lock was always a high point of the cruise. I still did not see the Boleys.

The second evening, we four foreigners and some of the crew were having a few at the bar. Bill expressed his concern about Mr. Boley, whose total isolation and rumors from the Chinese staff of heavy drinking boded ill. The last thing he or any of the Chinese working on board wanted was a sick and maybe dying passenger.

"We need to keep a watch on him. He looks in a bad way, though there's nothing in the passenger manifesto about any physical problems. I'll check with Doctor Yang."

Which was next to nothing. "I wonder if that will help much. Yang wouldn't know a hangnail from a hangover. Wasn't he a barefoot doctor in the Cultural Revolution?"

"So they say, but I want the Chinese involved in this as much as possible," Bill said, "in case anything goes wrong."

For the next couple of days, nothing much happened. I met with Amy the hostess, responsible for maintaining rooms and food preparation, and Lai Ming, Amy's assistant.

"My girls are worried about the people in Cabin 6," Lai Ming said. "They never go anywhere and leave the trash and dirty towels outside. The man won't even get up so they can change his bedding. And, they say it really stinks in there, even from outside."

"That's right," Amy said. "Neither of them has been down to eat. Everything's ordered through room service. A lot of the food is left in the corridor untouched, though we picked up some empty liquor bottles."

"What about Mrs. Boley," I asked. "How's she doing?"

"*Ma-ma hu-hu,*" so-so, Lai Ming said. "Whenever someone knocks on the door, she only opens it a little bit. She's nice to people, but very quiet and secretive."

"Any idea about his condition?" I asked.

"I think he sleeps a lot, and watches movies that he's had the staff borrow from the library." Amy said. "And drinks. That's about it."

I told Bill I'd check out Cabin 6. On the fourth afternoon, I rapped lightly on the door. Mrs. Boley inched it open, keeping the chain in place. I noted her inexpressive features, looking dowdy and frazzled, just as she had on arrival. I saw Mr. Boley supine on the bed, his eyes closed, mouth open, and making slight gurgling noises. He looked like a cadaver. I detected the odor of something like ether.

"Mrs. Boley, sorry to bother you, but we're concerned that you and Mr. Boley haven't been down to eat since you boarded. Is everything all right?"

"Oh, yes, just fine," she said in a monotone voice. "We're quite all right. My husband simply has a slight cold and he'd rather not be with the other passengers. The girls were very kind, bringing us sufficient victuals. And thank you for asking."

She backed into her room to close the door.

"Wouldn't you care to have the ship's doctor look at Mr. Boley?" I cringed at the "doctor" part, thinking it was like asking a barber to do a heart bypass.

"Oh, no, thank you. I'm sure he'll be all right. I will surely let you know if we need anything." She softly shut the door.

By the fifth day, and the sixth empty bottle of something called Sazerak Rye, I learned from Lai Ming's charges, in their all-too-brief encounters with Mrs. Boley that she apparently cleaned up after her husband, even when he failed to make it to the bathroom. The window curtains never opened, and Boley kept to his bed, only staring at the ceiling or the Bashan's videos or lying with his eyes closed.

I persisted with Bill to have Yang take a look, at least to confirm how Boley was doing, and to prevent any malpractice suits against either the ship's owners, which happened to be the Chinese government, or Lindblad, the American travel company. I doubted the good doctor could cure much, not here in the middle of the river, miles from even a small hamlet, but at least we needed to know.

"I agree," Bill said. "Let's talk to Mrs. Boley."

When we called at her suite and asked to speak with her, she pulled the door ajar as before. After we convinced her to meet with us, with some reluctance she released the chain and slipped through the narrow opening into the passageway, then shut the door quietly behind her. Her only makeup was a white powdery base that gave her face a drawn pasty look, and a thin line of lip rouge. She looked more haggard that I recalled on first seeing her. Her only jewelry was a simple gold wedding band.

"Yes?" she said, in her noncommittal voice.

"Mrs. Boley, I'm Bill Hurst, the cruise director of the *Bashan*. Sorry to bother you, but we, that is I and my staff, are worried about Mr. Boley's condition, and wonder if we might have him see our ship's physician, Dr. Yang. What do you think?"

She stood silent, hands clasped in front of her, wearing the same, or an identical gingham dress as the day she boarded. I tried to discern the facial features underneath the heavy layer of makeup. A high bridge, strong jawline, full lips. What really struck me is that her eyes, which appeared to have a dark beauty, instead looked droopy and dull. Had she worn a less severe garment, fixed her drab hair, and applied her cosmetics with more care—in other words, a complete makeover—she'd be a handsome woman instead of the mannikin in front of us.

"I don't know ... It's true he hasn't eaten much." She said this with downcast eyes, then raised them to look at Bill. "He doesn't have much of an appetite."

"I understand he's been drinking quite a lot," Bill said.

"It's normal for him. He always does, when he doesn't feel well. He thinks it helps him recover."

Bill's expression mirrored my own feelings of alarm. "Recover from what?"

Mrs. Boley fidgeted with her hands. "Well, he has a heart condition, you know."

"We didn't know that. I don't think it's mentioned in his medical statement."

I remembered looking it over and didn't recall any information on his physical condition, only that Boley was in his mid-70s, Mrs. Boley in her mid-50s. In any case, they both looked older than their years.

She seemed to search for what to say. "No, he was afraid if he put everything down that's wrong with him, he wouldn't be allowed to come on the trip." She was now wringing her hands, her head down, staring at the deck.

"Everything?"

"He sometimes gets shingles, and he has emphysema. I always told him not to smoke so much ... And his blood pressure, it gets pretty high. That's why he stays in bed so much."

"Mrs. Boley, this is serious. May we please have the doctor examine your husband?"

"Well, I don't know. I doubt my husband would like that."

"I'm sorry, but when a life may be in danger, it is the responsibility of the captain to be informed. Please, we must call the doctor."

Mrs. Boley nodded. "Very well. Let me know when. Oh, I do hope Jedidiah won't get too upset."

In half an hour, Dr. Yang cautiously entered Cabin 6. Mrs. Boley said she had given her husband an extra pill in hopes he would fall asleep. Otherwise, there might be quite a row.

I accompanied Yang to translate for him and saw for the first time Boley's vein-streaked hands and long, thin fingers and untrimmed nails that curled under, like talons—claws. They reminded me of a traditional Chinese gentry official whose fingernails sometimes grew into a loop of circles.

After taking as many readings as possible under the minimal shipboard conditions—temperature, blood pressure, pulse, drawn blood—Dr. Yang exited the cabin to meet with me, Bill, and Captain Wu.

"How is he?"

"His blood pressure very high, almost two hundred. Pulse … up and down."

"Fluctuating."

"Yes. Maybe more. I check his blood. Not good."

"Is he dying?" I asked.

Dr. Yang looked at Captain Wu, then at the rest of us. "Yes, I think so."

No one spoke.

"Can he make it to Chongqing?" Captain Wu asked.

"I don't know. If we hurry."

Bill turned to Captain Wu. "This is Friday. We're scheduled to arrive at Sunday noon. If we go full steam and do some night sailing, can we make it by tomorrow?"

I knew the last thing any of us wanted was to end up with a dead American on board. Captain Wu, short and stolid with a head of thick gray hair, nodded. "We will try, but night sailing on the Yangtze can be dangerous, and maybe illegal."

He decided we really had no choice. The whistlestops and villages along the shore to Chongqing had only the most meager facilities, if any at all. Our best option was to keep on to our home port. We sailed the rest of the day until near midnight before Captain Wu pulled up alongside a jetty at some nondescript shantytown, not wanting to push his luck. We tied up until the first hint of dawn about four o'clock, then resumed sailing.

On our final ascent, I looked over the Boleys' information forms required by any tourist operator.

> Names: Jedidiah Karl Boley, Sr. 76, and Edith Foster Boley, 56.
> Address: 7151 Oswald Avenue, Bend, Oregon.
> Occupation: Jedidiah Boley, retired. Edith Boley, housewife.
> Religion: Pentecostal.
> Dietary restrictions: None.

Under the long list of health problems, Mr. Boley showed only "Asthma." Mrs. Boley had ticked "None." According to the form, they were incredibly fit.

Finally, for Emergency Contact, both listed "No next of kin."

The *Bashan* docked just short of one o'clock on Saturday afternoon in Chongqing, China's most populous city.

As the Bashan's interpreter, I was the obvious one to accompany the Boleys to the hospital, not something I looked forward to. The Chinese crew included several bilingual Chinese, but Captain Wu insisted that an American be with Boley. While the ship was tying up, Bill and I went into the Boleys' room, now reeking of odors associated with hospitals that we learned emanated from Dr. Yang's medicine chest of prescriptions, and the rye.

None of the Chinese wanted anything to do with someone they were convinced was dying, so Bill and I set to, wrestling Boley onto a stretcher. We negotiated our burden, a six-foot skeleton of a man barely conscious, along an inner passageway to the gangplank and down to shore. We put Boley down to catch our breath, then made our way up a steep fifty-yard incline carrying the comatose figure in a typically heavy Chongqing fog. Visibility, a quarter mile.

At the top of an embankment, I heard the Changjiang—the Long River, the Yangtze—gurgle and plash in the distance. Mrs. Boley trudged beside us, wrapped in a heavy black greatcoat, saying nothing. It was impossible to read her feelings.

We reached an old Ford wood-paneled station wagon arranged for us to transport Boley to Chongqing Municipal Hospital Number One. We placed him in the back and lay a small blanket over him, leaving his bare feet exposed. In our haste, we'd forgotten his shoes. We didn't say anything to Mrs. Boley, and she seemed not to be aware. Bill returned to the *Bashan*.

After a twenty-minute ride through Chongqing's steep roads, reminiscent of San Francisco's, the Ford Country Squire that evoked incongruous memories of a Beach Boys woody, pulled in at the rear of the hospital, as gray and drab as the perpetual Chongqing overcast. Two attendants met us at the emergency entrance, worked Boley onto a gurney, and wheeled him to an elevator. The aides, Mrs. Boley, and I waited impatiently while the lift made a laboriously slow ascent. Not a word was spoken to us except to confirm Boley's identification, name and age. Aside from that and some whispering between the two attendants, all was silent.

When the elevator doors squeaked apart, the two aides rushed the gurney down several corridors, making left and right turns deeper into the maze, Mrs. Boley and I scurried after them. The dark dank concrete building was more than chilly—frigid—from an absence of any heating. In China, it's not turned on until November 1. Today was October 26.

Nor, apparently, the lighting. The only illumination issued through grimy windows.

We did not encounter a single other person. That fact I found off-putting. It happened to be Sunday, so maybe Chinese either don't get sick on weekends or they wait for the Sabbath to die.

It felt like a morgue. Parts of it probably were.

Our quintet continued turning corners and passing rooms on either side, their doors closed. The deadening quiet was foreboding. No doctors or nurses rushing about. No sounds. No nothing. I turned to see how Mrs. Boley was doing and found her dutifully plodding behind us, her face blank.

I kept glancing at Boley and wasn't sure he was alive. I had once worked in a mortuary and was familiar with how cadavers look. That was Boley: a skeletal face, sunken eyes, colorless lips, waxy gray skin, and the odor of death about him.

The aides and their gurney made a sudden stop at one of the doors. One aide opened it while the other wheeled Boley into a small room barely large enough for a surgical table, a smattering of hospital equipment, and three women in white smocks who stood together against one wall.

Immediately, they jumped to transfer Boley onto the table and took to arranging and preparing various instruments. Mrs. Boley had remained outside the examination room and did not see the doctors remove Boley's shirt, affix the oxygen mask, and insert an IV tube.

One of the women asked me to please take Mrs. Boley down the hall to an area that served as a waiting room, where we found a chair and a bus-stop bench. She sat on the bench, straight and prim as a young pupil from a clapboard-siding one-room prairie schoolhouse waiting for the schoolmarm to appear.

She docilely declined when I asked if she would like some water or something else. I retrieved a glass of water anyway. She sat demurely with her usual bland expression, toying with a white linen handkerchief embroidered delicately with magenta and yellow flowers. I felt sorry for her and sat as silent as she. Nothing I could do, nothing to say. Only wait.

Periodically, I checked in on Boley. None of the doctors said anything to me, didn't even look up when I went in, engrossed in attending to him and speaking only in brief low comments to each other. After some time conferring and checking gauges, they began tapping, then pushing, and finally beating on his chest. The next time I went in, they were standing around him, observing the body as if willing it to live.

Three hours after we were admitted, one of the doctors looked at me. "*Ta si-le.*"

He's dead.

Part 2

My first words to the doctors were gratuitous. "*Ni chweding?*" You're sure?

"*Mei wenti.*" No question about it.

Now what? First, I had to tell the new widow. She sat immobile, as she had the entire three hours. When I approached her, she gave a wan smile, and nodded. "I know."

"I'm very sorry, Mrs. Boley. Are you all right? I mean, there are some formalities we'll have to take care of. Can you manage that?"

"Of course. Just tell me what to do."

How could she be so polite and accommodating? Talk about cool or maybe just numb.

"I can handle most of the paperwork with the doctors. But there is one thing they need to know immediately: How to deal with the body."

I kicked myself for being so blunt, but she took it stoically. I explained to her the three options—burial, cremation, or removal of the body to another country—and that the third was extremely difficult and costly and very time consuming.

Without hesitation, she replied, "Oh, cremation. We've already decided on that." It almost seemed they had planned for Boley to die in China though I took it as a general decision.

I conferred with the chief nurse. There would be no autopsy. Nor had Mrs. Boley asked for one.

I walked her back to the station wagon and gave the driver instructions to the hotel. Driving Chongqing's cobblestone streets, Mrs. Boley stared out the window. What was she thinking?

Just then, she heaved a deep sigh and turned to look at me. "You know, from now on I won't have to turn off my bed lamp at night when I read. Jedidiah would not tolerate that bed light." She said this as if punctuating a "so there."

I wondered where that came from.

Just short of six o'clock we arrived at Chongqing's newest accommodation, the Yangtze Mansions. Even so, it was the typical Chinese affair, maybe or maybe not three stars by Western standards. At least the rooms were still clean without the usual carpet stains and faulty lighting, and they all had private baths. I checked her into one and took another for myself.

I saw her to her room and asked her if was hungry and wanted to see the dining room. She said not very and no, preferring to keep to her room. I hadn't eaten since breakfast. My stomach was growling, but after the day's momentous events, I didn't feel much like eating either. I, too, preferred to eat alone.

I made sure her luggage was delivered. Since I lived on board the *Bashan*, all my belongings were there. I explained to her that I had to get to the ship and pick up some things before the *Bashan* left the dock and anchored at a buoy in the river until Monday's departure.

"During that time I'll be on hand should you need anything."

I told her that the next day would be a busy one. I had to report Boley's demise to the US Consulate. I also had to purchase a ticket for Mrs. Boley's return flight to the States since she had no intention of continuing on with the group. And I had to arrange for the cremation, to which she would have to accompany me.

"Are you okay with that?" I asked.

"Whatever must be done, must be done. You've been very kind and most helpful. I can't do much, but I hope you will feel free to take any of Jedidiah's clothing that you'd like. I can't use any of his things and I'm not taking them back."

I wasn't up to wearing a dead man's clothes, but I could dispose of them later.

"What time tomorrow should I be ready?"

"Once I finish at the consulate and the airline office, I'll pick you up. Say about noon." I was about to leave, then stopped to ask where she wanted to fly.

"Los Angeles is best, I think."

"That's an awful long way from Oregon. Not Portland or San Francisco?"

"No, LA is fine."

I spent several hours the next morning negotiating a plane ticket in China where queues are unknown, and where the consulate proved to be predictably bureaucratic. My timing was about right, and I finished the business just short of noon, and straightaway returned to the hotel with a good deal of misgiving. I didn't look forward to keeping company with a one-day widow at a cremation.

Dutifully, she was waiting in the lobby, dressed in black. It was a somber ride to the Chongqing Crematorium Number Eleven.

A man in an ill-fitting suit showed us into a waiting room with sofas and chairs, a shelf of urns, ubiquitous silk flowers, and the unavoidable smell of formaldehyde. Mrs. Boley sat on a sofa, sedate and distant, while I spoke with the director. He assured me that Mr. Boley's corpse had been delivered. He asked that Mrs. Boley select an urn of her choice, and that I must, as Mrs. Boley's representative, witness the cremation.

She took her time looking over the models and photographs of a couple of dozen urns. She settled on an egg-shaped celadon piece, black with purple and pink azaleas, and paid the equivalent of forty dollars in Chinese currency. That done, Mr. Chen led me across an expanse of dirt, past rows of real flowers to a separate building, while Mrs. Boley remained in the waiting lounge.

I entered a small plain room that held the body of Jedidiah Boley. Two middle-aged guys dressed in casual street wear, stood talking and giggling, playing grab-ass and playfully punching each other. They acted like school kids but looked to be in their 50s.

Boley was dressed as I'd first seen him in his flannel shirt and denims. He didn't have the waxy look that otherwise comes with embalming but held the same unrelentingly grim visage. You SOB, I thought, you finally got your comeuppance. I felt for Mrs. Boley, thinking of her alone in a cold room waiting for her late husband's ashes.

After I identified the body, they insisted on having my picture taken with the cadaver. They positioned me close to it with my hand on his shoulder—like pals—and I wore a shit-eating grin. They took turns flashing their camera. I almost expected old Boley to start laughing.

That done, they wheeled his gurney to yet another building housing three crematories. When we reached the middle one and opened the door, I saw then felt a white-hot blast. They skillfully moved the body onto a roller bed that jutted out, pushed him—or it—inside, and shut the door. They told me it takes about ninety minutes to complete, and that I should return to the waiting area.

Mrs. Boley conducted herself with aplomb throughout the entire ordeal. I was agitated, feeling that I should do something to ease her burden. I felt like reaching out to her but checked that impulse. She must have noticed my discomfort and turned to me. "I'm fine, I really am. Not to worry."

The ninety minutes seemed as many hours.

After returning to the hotel, I took Boley's things and retired to my room, exhausted after days of dealing with dying and death. Still, I couldn't put away a nagging sense of guilt. I wondered what it must be like for a now single, homespun woman, light years away from her home in eastern Oregon, adrift in a foreign place, no apparent living relatives, with no one or nowhere to turn.

At that point, my only thought was to crash on the inviting bed in my room, but guilt overcame desire.

At seven o'clock, I picked up the phone and asked Mrs. Boley if she wanted to dine with me.

"I'd love to. Thank you so much."

Her surprisingly lively response caught me off-guard. I was pleased—and puzzled—to hear her respond with such high spirit. That was fast.

I stopped by her room and knocked on the door.

"Yes, what is it?" I heard her call out.

"Mrs. Boley, do you still want to have dinner?"

"Of course. I just need a few minutes. I'll meet you in the restaurant."

"Very well." I turned and went down to the dining area, where about half of the thirty or so tables were occupied, mostly by white foreigners—likely tourists and businessmen—and some Chinese—likely all businessmen. I picked a table away from the main groups, thinking Mrs. Boley might prefer a quieter setting.

When the waitress brought me a menu, I explained I was waiting for another guest. I asked if she had a wine list. No wine list. That didn't surprise me. But what did is that the hotel restaurant had any wine at all. Four choices. Three were Chinese, one a French selection I'd never heard of, and figured it was left there by a departing tourist from Paris. I said I would wait for my guest before deciding.

I'd been sitting for about ten minutes, looking over the simple décor, mostly copies of scrolls of Tang, Sung, and Ming paintings, and calligraphy examples from famous poets and literati, all hanging on dull whitewashed walls. Standard for a tourist hotel. I sat, lulled by the buzz of conversation. My dozing was abruptly interrupted by a sudden silence. I looked up and saw across the room the dim outline of a figure walking toward my table.

I watched a woman materialize as she drew near.

Good God!

I rose, my mind reeling, watching a most comely and chic woman approaching my table. Whatever had happened to Edith Boley?

She wore not mourning black, but a knee-length cocktail dress, in pale blue, pulled in at the waist with a white, shiny, patent leather belt, and not a little décolletage. What looked like a silk Navy blue shawl covered her shoulders. She had combed out and fixed her frizzy hair into a tight chignon. She laughed at my dumbfounded look.

"Good evening. I apologize for being late."

"Um…not at all." I stood stupefied. "You are Mrs. Boley? You look…marvelous."

"Thank you. I think Jedidiah would approve. Don't you think?"

"Yes, I'm sure he would." How could he not?

I moved around the table and pulled the chair out for her, something I'd not done for a hundred years. Seating a lady—whoa.

I took my seat and asked if she'd like something to drink.

"Do they have wine here?"

"Barely. It's mostly Chinese which I do not recommend, and one French which probably isn't very good."

"Let's try the French, shall we?"

I agreed and continued to ogle her. What the hell was going on?

The waitress brought and opened a bottle of Chateau La Croix de Pietet, 1976, which meant nothing to me. She left the bottle on the table without serving it. I looked at Mrs. Boley, and both of us raised our eyebrows.

"Welcome to China," I said while I poured us a small sample.

We toasted our drinks. A number of guests were still watching us.

Edith Boley knew her wine etiquette. She picked up her goblet, tipped it away from her to observe its true color and whether it was cloudy or clear. She followed this with the swirl and sniff ritual, and to note the legs or the way the wine ran back down inside the glass. "Well, here goes," she said, and took a generous taste that she swished around her mouth. She held it a moment then swallowed and looked at me.

"What do you think, Mrs. Boley?"

She placed the goblet on the table. "Not the best," she said. "The nose is cooked, and the palate's too tart, so is the finish. It really has no body. What about you?"

"I'm used to the diesel fuel in China, but this is a lot better than their damson plum wine. That'll pucker you up, for sure."

She laughed. "Call it an adventure. And please, no more 'Mrs. Boley.' Call me Veronica."

Veronica?

It became obvious Mrs. Boley was not all that she'd seemed. "What happened to Edith?"

"There never was an Edith. Nor a Mrs. Boley. At least, not me."

"Should I ask what this is all about? Or is it better left unsaid?"

She took a sip of her wine, then put the goblet aside. "No more of that" she said. "Now that the charade is over, I don't mind telling you."

I knew I should desist and forget the whole business. But my curiosity proved too powerful. I had to know.

"Over? You mean Mr. Boley death?"

"Yes, it's all done."

"Well, if I may," I said, "how long have you, or had you known him?"

"I first laid eyes on him six weeks ago, though we were in communication by letter and phone for several months."

I started to have some queasy feelings about this. "Okay, so it sounds like you did a bit of planning."

"I'll explain. Jedidiah had no family, no living relatives that he knew of, or so he told me. At least no one whom he wanted to leave his estate to."

I nodded, starting to form a picture.

"Until about a year ago, he was in fair health, lived alone, and didn't have much of a life. He'd never developed any hobbies or sports, nothing to take up his spare time. He had plenty of money, but nowhere to spend it."

"Until you came along?"

Veronica smiled. "Nothing quite like that. In fact, he hasn't spent a penny on me. But I have fulfilled a role."

"As his wife."

"Not exactly. All those ailments I mentioned to you were true. He had a whole list of physical problems, most of them incurable. It really was only a matter of time, a very short time until he was certain to die. And he didn't want to die alone in a sleepy little town in the Oregon outback. He decided he wanted what he called a helpmate, a last hurrah. That's where I came in."

We sat back when the waitress brought our dinner.

"He made it clear he didn't want me in Bend. He managed to take care of himself until a month ago. He was still ambulatory but getting very weak. That's when we decided to meet in Portland, where I took over."

"That all seems fairly straight forward, but…well, what about the marriage?"

"That was my call. I agreed to do whatever it took, whatever he wanted from the time we met in person until he died. He explained his lack of any heir, and that he didn't want to turn over his wealth to anyone, including a charity, he didn't know personally. I was it."

"Was he wealthy?"

"Very. I've reviewed all his papers, and his will. He's worth a million, a couple of times over."

I raised my eyebrows. "Wow, lucky you."

"Yes, and lucky him. I like to think of it as a win-win situation. Each of us got something we wanted, we broke no laws, and we're both better off."

I agreed that it sounded reasonable. "Congratulations. And I'm not being sarcastic. By the way, how did he make his money?"

"He worked the rodeo circuit, bronc busting, calf roping, bull riding. He started in his teens, it was his life, though it broke more bones than he could count. When he got too old, and he said he rode until he was over fifty, he invested and owned his own rodeo. Made a lot of money, most of it from TV contracts."

I had stuck with my wine and called the waitress over to ask about scotch. I needed that.

"This is fascinating, but can I ask you another question?"

She nodded. "Certainly."

"How did you meet him if you never laid eyes on him until six weeks ago?"

She glanced down then looked directly at me. "I'll tell you something. For anyone interested, it's quite easy to find people in his condition. Old people who have no family, no friends, and a lot of money. The thing is to read the dating ads, where so many people seek a partner. After a while, you begin to recognize patterns and can tell when someone, like Jedidiah, wants a final companion. Then you start to communicate first by mail, then by phone. Quite easy you know."

"This is fascinating, but another thing. If you've never lived with him, what was the comment about the reading light?"

She smiled. "Simply part of the script. I love to embellish. Everything I told you is true." She drew in a deep breath. "It may seem mercenary, but as I explained, it was win-win. I don't feel the least bit guilty."

"No, the way you put it, there's nothing wrong."

She looked at me. "You probably don't believe that, but my conscience is clear."

The waitress brought a bottle of Glenlivet, also probably left by a passing tourist. I looked at Veronica and held up the bottle. "May I?"

"By all means."

"Water or ice?"

"Neat, thank you."

We clinked our glasses and took long draughts.

"I suppose what really stumps me is—why China? Of all places in the world, this seems so out of the way."

"That's why. I've done research on these cases, and it's better to be in countries with a weak legal system, and where the government is not inclined to delve too deeply into a foreigners' affairs. Simply take care of the situation, and wave goodbye, no questions asked."

"These cases? There are others?"

She nodded. "This was my fourth. The first time I accompanied a gentleman to Belarus. Another to Serbia. Then once to Paraguay. And now, China."

"You've made a career of it? Astounding."

"No, it's more of a sideline, an avocation."

"What's your real profession then?"

She tilted her head and looked at me coyly. "I thought you'd have guessed that by now. I'm an actress," she said, holding out her glass. "Salut."

COLORBLIND

Part 1

Los Angeles, CA, 1963

August 31, 1962, was a red-letter day for me. That's when I completed a four-year commitment in the US Air Force earning an honorable discharge—barely.

I moved to Los Angeles to find work and continue my education. I'd saved close to a thousand dollars working the black market during my two-year stint in Turkey. Those savings helped me get started until I found a job with the California Department of Motor Vehicles where I worked the swing shift. Easy life, no stress. Perfect for a college student at LA City College. The job was all phone work. I answered calls from law enforcement offices that gave me car license numbers to look up from a massive data base like a giant library card catalogue. In return, I provided information from the registration forms: names, addresses, phone numbers, all that.

In short order, I came to know several callers without ever seeing them. One in particular, Cynthia Banks, worked with the LAPD on the same swing shift. On slower nights we found time to chat it up.

We hit it off early on. Cynthia was easy to talk to, had a sexy voice and a nice laugh. I always looked forward to her calls. Since we were both single, unattached, and in our mid-twenties, it didn't take me long to ask her out. We set a time for Saturday night. She gave her address, 1120 East Adams Boulevard, the King's Arms Apartments, 12B.

I didn't pay much attention to where she lived until I drove there. East Adams wasn't Beverly Hills. It wasn't Boyle Heights either. It's a motley bunch of whites, Blacks, Latinos, and Asians. With all the gang activity, East Adams is where you're better off not going out after nine o'clock, or not going out at all. As I neared her address, I fell into second thoughts, torn between going ahead, and turning back. My imagination and unfamiliarity with mixed neighborhoods conjured all sorts of bad scenes. But Cynthia seemed so together and energetic, I kept on driving.

I had to park a couple of blocks away from her place, where I noticed four big dudes hanging out, smoking, horsing around. They stopped and glared when I walked past. I pretended to be nonchalant and strolled on by. When they heckled me, I picked up the pace. They went back to playing grab-ass.

The King's Arms, like all the other apartments in the neighborhood, was a two-story block, U-shaped around a swimming pool. The complex wasn't gated. "Gated" in South Central LA meant only one thing: prison. I walked through the open entrance, checked the locater: B apartments, second floor. A few folks stood around chatting it up, watching others frolicking in the pool. They glanced up, then went on with their poolside jiving.

I climbed to the second level, and walked half-way down the balcony to apartment 12B, knocked a couple of raps on the door, wondering who would open it. I hadn't given any thought to Cynthia's ethnic identity, just didn't matter. Besides, I hadn't noticed anything, even the way she talked, to make me think she wasn't white, just like me. Now I noticed.

I heard a thunk from the dead bolt, the door pulled open, and there she stood. Whoops. I turned so tongue-tied I couldn't even muster "hello." C'mon brain, do something. She waited a few seconds, got the picture, and started laughing. A delightful laugh, full of mirth and fun and not ridiculing.

My initial impression of her was feline, a taller, darker version of the kittenish Eartha Kitt. The catlike eyes, impish mouth, perky expression. She stood a couple of inches short of my six feet, a hand on her hip, as if daring me.

Once she squared the circle of my gaffe, she gave a flirty look at me standing there, still dumbfounded.

"Well, would you like to come in?"

"Uh, sure." I took a step toward the door. "You are Cynthia Banks?"

"I'd better be, I'm paying her bills. Nice to meet you," she said, holding out her hand. We shook. I entered, and immediately felt at home.

She'd decorated her otherwise cookie-cutter apartment with cultivated taste. Aside from the stock kitchen linoleum, her pad reflected Cynthia's composed personality. Stylish chrome art-deco furniture complemented eclectic prints that added color and cool. She walked me through a couple of French masters—Manet and Sereut—a Klee and a Picasso, and a pair of modernist sculptures. A Buddha statue on a teak stand, and a number of carvings and jewelry I assumed from Africa and Asia graced pieces of furniture that definitely weren't from Sears.

Then I noticed another work standing alone, a portrait sitting on an easel. Cynthia? Or maybe not. At first glance, I found the mood it evoked unsettling, even disturbing. The more I studied it, the more I perceived different layers, or perspectives. I looked over at Cynthia, standing off, her arms crossed. Challenging.

Her expression, like the painting, was enigmatic. For a moment, she and her portrait portrayed the same bifurcated personality, a twin, a doppelgänger.

I looked again at the picture. Provocative. No—more than that—surreal. The eyes vacant yet penetrating, the lips caught between a smile and a taunt, the face…a haunting expression.

I felt myself pulled in, deep, like the weightlessness of being underwater. "Dorian Grey" I mumbled to myself and felt a chill. "Is that you?"

Still in the same pose, she said, "Sometimes. What do you think?"

I stared at the painting as if it had an answer. "It's unreal. Who painted it?"

"I did, a self-portrait."

"It's incredible. I could view this all day. Definitely good enough to exhibit. Why the hell are you working for the police?"

"It's called making a living. Earning income as an artist has the same odds as winning at Vegas."

"Then go. From my angle, I'd say you are pretty damned accomplished. Blows me away."

"Bless you." She dippped a curtsy in a faux bow.

When I finished admiring her art work, she indicated a seat and sat down next to me, her legs together at an angle. "Are you over your shock?" she asked.

"It showed, did it? Sorry, I wasn't expecting you."

She grinned. "What were you expecting?" she said.

I stumbled over an answer. "Something white."

She laughed. "You want to bow out? It won't bother me." She drew a coy look as if she knew very well I wouldn't.

She was right. "Cynthia, I'm staying right here."

"Fair enough, make yourself comfortable. What can I get you to drink?"

"I'll have what you have."

"Typical man, no imagination. It's beer, wine, or spirits. Or all three."

"Wine."

"Red or white?"

"Red. You sure have a full bar."

"Always ready for the big one."

What was that supposed to mean?

In the kitchen, ten feet away, she asked, "Ever dated a Black woman before?"

"No, I knew a few in high school, but never went out with one."

"Why not?" I heard the pop of a cork, then liquid pouring.

"I don't know, no reason. Dated Mexicans and Japanese though." I recalled the fun times I'd had with Arlene de la Cruz and Suzie Matsuda.

"Ooo, so I'm the first one, she said, returning with two goblets of red. She placed them on the coffee table. "I'll get us some chips and dip."

"You ever date a white guy?"

"Not here in LA, just good friends," she said from the kitchen.

"Where then?"

She returned with munchies. I held out my drink in a toast. We clinked glasses. "In Chicago where I'm from," she said.

"Chicago. You any relation to Ernie Banks?" I asked, sipping my drink.

"He's my cousin."

I stared at her. "Really? Ernie Banks, baseball's Number One, is your cousin?"

"Ever since I was born."

"Is he as cool as you?"

"Nobody's that cool." She smiled, took a long draft. "You said on the phone once you were in the Air Force, in Texas."

"Right, Lackland AFB. What a hole, but it got worse when I shipped out to Keesler for more training."

"Where's Keesler?"

"Biloxi, Mississippi. Ever been there?"

"Deep South, sure, but not to Biloxi. I took part in a couple of civil rights marches, in Georgia and Alabama.

King is planning a really big one to DC in August. I'm thinking of going. What did you think of Biloxi?"

"Wasn't for me. Just never got used to all the separation of whites and Blacks, you know, restrooms, drinking fountains, ice cream parlors. I didn't grow up like that."

"That's why we're marching," she said, studying her cupped hands holding the goblet. "Ever have any problems in Biloxi?"

"Once, but not with Black people. In 1959, I wanted to see the Mardi Gras in New Orleans. Threw on my civvies and went out to wait for a bus. They were all packed, several passed by, so when I finally got to board one it was SRO. Except for an empty seat in the rear. A few whites were standing up front and I figured they were getting off at the next stop."

Cynthia put on a wry smile. She saw where this was going.

"I thought heck with it, and headed down the aisle for that seat. Every time I passed a row, the people sitting there stared up at me like I was a zombie. When I took that empty seat all of them, everyone aboard, including the driver, turned around gawking at me. I thought maybe I'd forgotten to zip up or that I'd shortchanged the coin box.

"For a full two minutes, the whole bus just stared at me. An old Black guy in the seat across from me had a big grin on. No one said a word, after awhile some turned around to face front, the driver too, who shifted into low, and we took off."

"Then what?" Cynthia asked.

"Nothin', but by the time we got to New Orleans, it hit me what I'd done. Whites in front, Blacks in the rear. Broke the Eleventh Commandment. The hell with it. I never grew up with those kind of rules, and wasn't about to follow them. Sure was an eyeopener, though."

She noticed my empty glass. "Refill?"

"You bet."

She returned with our drinks and a pensive look. "Did that bother you?"

"For sure, but I felt bad for the colored…sorry, I mean for the Negroes, too. It just doesn't make sense to me. I'm not the greatest do-gooder ever, but I don't get how people can think like that. Ever since that happened, I've had a different view of the South."

"You're Black, you get used to it."

"Shouldn't have to," I said.

We chatted through our second round. Feeling a buzz, I asked Cynthia if she wanted to take a ride, get a bite to eat.

She gave me a coy look. "You're not afraid of being out there with a Black woman?"

I felt pretty good, but the question stopped me. California, where I was born and raised, was always left-of-center, considered a Northern state in the American Civil War a hundred years ago. But even here, in 1963, *nobody* went that far. Whites dating Blacks just wasn't done. In half of America, you'd be ostracized. In the other half, you'd land in jail or the morgue. But here and now, for whatever reason, her ethnicity didn't bother me. Didn't even register. I liked her for who she was, her personality, her style. Her color be damned, and I had to admit ebony was a turn-on.

"Hey, let's paint the town red, as they say."

We went downstairs to the bright red MGB roadster I'd bought with a down payment from my blackmarket money. "You want to put the top down?"

"Put it down," she said, "so people can see what a neat couple we are."

Her remark put me on cloud nine. Took thirty seconds to create a convertible.

The first test came when we pulled into a service station to gas up. The attendant was a skinny white kid, about twenty, who sauntered over. When he saw us, he stopped, did a double take, looked around as if not sure what to do. He finally decided we were real people.

"Yessir, what can I do for ya?" he asked, staring at Cynthia, then at me, back to her.

"Fill it with regular."

"Yessir."

"While you're at it, how about the windshield."

"Yessir."

Cynthia and I chatted while the kid went about his work. When he started on the glass, he couldn't take his eyes off her, and kept wiping the same spot, over and over.

"Careful, you'll rub a hole in it," she said, throwing him a sexy smile.

"Yessir…er, ma'am. Sure don't want that to happen."

He hopped to. I paid him. As we drove off, I saw him in the mirror, standing there, still staring at us.

"You sure yanked his chain," I said. "He'll be telling his buddies all over town."

"Maybe we'll be famous," Cynthia said, pursing her lips.

I glanced her way. She seemed dead serious but for the wrong reasons. "Where to?" I said, turning onto Wilshire Boulevard.

"Ever been to Dino's?"

"Driven past it. Looks pretty nice. Think they'll let us in?"

"Let's find out," she said, as if challenging the place.

We pulled into the rear lot where an attendant, another scrawny type, lounged around, watching the cars. When we drove into an empty space, the guy came and made a visual inspection.

"Sorry, sir, this slot's reserved. You'll have to park outside."

"On the street?"

"Yessir, on the street."

I looked at Cynthia. She shrugged. Her former cool had turned icy.

We parked across the street.

When we entered, I saw why they called it Dino's. The background music was all Dean Martin's crooning. Paintings and photos, some of Dean alone, others with famous stars and politicos, papered the walls.

The dim lighting was designed to appeal to upscale folks, a place where a social climber takes his date to say "Yes."

We were met by a beefcake host and glamour girl hostess, most likely college kids, trying to impress a higher-class clientele. The woman was a little slip of a thing, blonde, trying to appear sophisticated as she lurched around in five-inch spiked heels, two inches too high.

The galoot reminded me of Lana Turner's bodyguard-lover, Johnny Stompanato. A typical mob gangster, the type who wore tailored sharkskin suits over a flowery Hawaiian silk shirt unbuttoned down to his navel. He wore a gold chain around his neck, and enough rings to open a jewelry store. His name said it all—*Stomp*anato. Except Lana's fourteen-year-old daughter stabbed him to death when he got rough with mommy.

This Johnny asked Cynthia and me to take a seat in the entryway where we waited for a table. Twenty minutes and four couples later, we got the picture.

"This ever happen to you before, Cynthia?"

"Sometimes."

"Want to go?"

"Sure…wait a sec."

Uh oh. I got the foreboding she was about to do something crazy. Watching her, I envisioned her handling guys bigger than myself. Get her dander up, and she could be a handful.

Like now.

Mr. Maitre d' had just greeted couple number five with "Follow me, please," and turned to lead them to a table. That's when Cynthia rose to her full height, raised her chin in disdain, and slid in between him and the couple.

"Hello, baby," Cynthia breathed, soft and seductive, ignoring the couple behind her. "Remember me? LaBelle LaBeau? Sure you do."

The guy spun around to face her only inches apart. His bowl-sized eyes said it all, astonishment plastered on his face. He tried to back away, but she kept pace, making salacious sighs. "Why didn't you come back? You said you would. Don't you want me?" She put her hand on the back of his neck to pull him closer, reached up to muss his thick wavy hair.

The whole act was so corny, I couldn't believe she was getting away with it. Her audacity had everyone off balance. I worried some of the customers might get aggressive. On the contrary, people began to titter, then laugh out loud. Everyone watched with rapt attention to see where this was headed.

Cynthia was in the groove. She tightened her hold on his neck, shifted to a more threatening whisper loud enough to be heard above Dean's crooning. "Listen, you cracker, I don't cotton to being treated like the trash you let into this place. You broke your promise, so you pay the price. See you in court!"

She pulled her hand down to pinch his earlobe and twist it. He yelled and grabbed the side of his head. With that, she turned on her heel and stormed out. I followed, barely able to keep a straight face.

When we got back to the car, I sat back without starting the engine. Cynthia needed to cool down.

"You okay?"

She nodded. "I'll be fine."

I considered her performance. "You were fantastic, Cynthia."

She raised an eyebrow. "It comes from practice."

"You should get an Oscar for Best Actress."

"I wasn't acting," she said.

She didn't say anything more right away. Then she turned to me, and we embraced in the open-air MG at the corner of Westwood and Wilshire, one of the country's busiest intersections. When we moved apart, she looked hard at me, daring. "If you want to take me home, I understand," she said.

"No way, but I'll bet you gave that guy a cauliflower ear."

She laughed.

I reached over to squeeze her hand. "C'mon, let's get something to eat. Tell me where."

"You ready for some down-home southern fare?"

"I repeat, tell me where to go."

"Turn down Manchester and head for Normandy. I'll show you the way."

So, on our first date, we leisurely attended to hushpuppies, fried catfish, sautéed okra, and peach cobbler at the N'awlins Grill. To top it off, no one gave a hoot who we were, or what colored clay we were made of. Just folks, until…

I sat back savoring the peach cobler with brandy when I noticed a large black cloud hovering over Cynthia with a hand on her shoulder—to steady himself.

"Hey, baby, long time no mix. Missed ya. So, who's your friend here, have we met?" The black cloud spoke to her but looked at me who stared back at the pinpoint droopy eyes.

For the second time that night, she stiffened, trying to ward off another inconvenience. "Okay, Aldi, this is my friend, we work together on the night shift—"

"I don' go for this night shift business." Now he looked directly at me, the newcomer. "Maybe time for you to vacate."

I made a move to confront Aldi when Cynthia cut him off, throwing him a decidedly mean look. "Don't you go tellin' my friends what to do, Aldi. I'll see who I want. Go find somebody else."

Still looking at me, he spoke to her. "Yes, indeed, Miss Banks, sho' don' wanna upset the cart." He shifted his attention. "Let's just say the next time I see you," he stabbed a finger at me, "you better be someone else. Get my meaning, cracker?" He pulled away and shuffled toward the entrance, bumping into a chairs and tables on his way out. So long, Aldi.

Part 2

Over the next few months, Cynthia and I grew close. At times, we discussed if we were in love, or "falling" in love, then let it go because neither of us knew what that meant.

One evening, Cynthia said she'd like to take me to a friend's birthday party. "You still haven't met any of my circle. Time's up."

"Sounds good. Who's your friend?"

"Ronnie Smith. His date is Natalie Cole. Ever heard of her?"

"Cole as in Nat King Cole?"

"Her papa."

"You sure swim in rich waters. Ernie Banks, Natalie Cole. Who else?"

"You might meet some bright lights at the party. Not sure who'll be there."

"What's the occasion?"

"Ronnie's birthday. I think he's all of nineteen. Younger than the rest of us, but people like him. And, it's nice to have Natalie join us. She's a kick. Has a great voice if we can get her to sing."

Ronnie lived in a simple apartment, similar to Cynthia's though without her taste in décor. For this bash, they'd taken over the clubhouse and outdoor grill area.

When we arrived at eight, the party had already shifted into high gear. A generous buffet ran along one wall, and two bbqs were in full heat to serve the thirty or forty guests who kept coming and going. A trio of Ronnie's friends formed a jazz combo, with occasional songs by Natalie and another girl, Wendy Wilson. The whole affair reached a fever pitch from a cascade of alcohol.

Cynthia introduced me to Ronnie and Natalie and a few of the others, big guys who resembled bulldozers. I wasn't the smallest fellow in town, but these dudes made me look it. They could easily play offensive tackle for the Chicago Bears. Maybe some of them did.

At least forty people eventually showed up. I was the only white one.

After we mixed it up with several of Cynthia's friends, she angled away to meet with another group. I finished my beer and wandered off to grab a refill. Standing away from the crowd, I watched several couples dancing free style to their own steps, from jitterbug to the Watusi, the Twist to Locomotion. Man, they really had the moves, like they were created by a different potter. I never saw white people go through such twists and bends.

Cynthia returned. "You dance?"

He pointed to the couples. "Not like that."

"C'mon, I'll show you."

And she did. I thought I could cut it pretty well, but Cynthia had me all over the place. After a few songs I wanted to call it quits when Natalie agreed to sing the torch song "Cry Me a River," made famous by Julie London.

I wiped my brow. "Now that one I can do."

"Stick around," she said. "We'll get you up to speed." She excused herself again, leaving me to finish my drink.

Reginald—"Reggie"—a tall gangly type, wandered over. I held a can of Brew 102, a local LA product. Cheap and flat, but worth every bit of the dollar eighty-five for a six pack. We chatted it up, sports, movies, music.

"You with Cynthia? She's a corker. Hep, man."

I figured Reggie was talking positive.

"She's spot on, all right."

Reggie wrinkled his brow. "Spot on?"

"Tops."

"You with Cynthia, you at the top. Stay there."

"Treat her like a soul sister."

"Better'n that, man."

"Yeah, better."

Reggie saluted with his beer can and moved off, followed by Dee Dee who sidled over. "Reg given' you the stiff?"

"No problem. Just watching out for Cynthia."

"Cynthia can take care of herself. It's Reg who needs work. But I'm glad you're with her. You got the jive, man."

"Thanks, Dee Dee. It's good comin' from you."

"You're in the groove. Any time you want to hang out, just come on by. We got room for one more." She reached up and pecked me on the cheek. "Dig?"

"Dig."

Throughout the evening, a few more of Cynthia's friends engaged with me. As woozy wobbly drunk as some of the Green Bay tackles were, none made any obnoxious moves. No snide remarks or challenges. No one out to prove anything. I hadn't considered what they'd think about this whitey dating one of their own. Seemed they didn't care. It was up to me and Cynthia.

A couple of guys joked over it, but not threateningly. In fact, the jokes were okay, on the corny side. Stuff like, "Hey, Brad, know how to find Cynthia in the dark? Tickle her feet, and she'll scream." I laughed with them, not at the joke, but at their own boisterous hilarity.

Around ten, a trio of guys joined in. One of them was Aldi. When I saw them I smelled the deep end of bad. They were "spaded," a word I thought I'd heard before, maybe in the Air Force. Hard to keep up with the slang. In short, they were drunk. Sloppy drunk. Aldi wove through clusters of guests, bumping into some, as he headed for the beer barrel to grab two bottles. One for himself and the other for himself.

One of Cynthia's friends, Greg, told me not to pay any attention to Aldritch "Aldi" Gates. Right, except how do you ignore two-hundred-fifty pounds of inebriation?

"I already met Aldi. I don't think he likes me."

"He don' like any whiteys," Dee Dee came in. "Aldi can have a short fuse. Looks like he's flowin' tonight. He has this thing, you see. His brother was shot, killed by a white cop. Anytime he sees a Black woman with a honky, he makes it personal. Besides, he was datin' Cynthia when you came along."

He looked at Cynthia. "Is that right?"

She shrugged. "Doesn't matter. I make my own friends."

"Heey," Aldi approached Cynthia and me. "Look what we got here." At least he wasn't soused enough not to recognize me.

From ten yards away, Aldi, with his entourage in tow, pushed through the crowd like a snowplow creating a path through the forest to stand in front of me, which for my part wished this goon would disappear. I never feared a drunk, too uncoordinated to do much. Even so, Aldi looked harder than a boulder, although I was pretty solid after all the weightlifting I'd done in the Air Force, now a cut above two-ten. Size wasn't the problem. I didn't want to do anything to embarrass Cynthia or compromise her friends. I'd see where Aldi took this.

One of Cynthia's crowd, Willie, tried to defuse the intoxicated moose. That, too, bothered me, I didn't want to rely on someone else to settle my problems. Neither did I want to get the crap beat out of me.

"Okay, Aldi," Willie said "you made your point, why not just turn around and we'll see you later. Grab a six-pack on your way out."

I was pretty sure that wouldn't work.

"Hey, man, this is me and this…" Aldi paused, "this, this white goose." He broke up over his own stupid joke. "Hey, we got enough problems with the fuzz. Don' need another one. Who asked him here anyway?"

"I did," Cynthia broke in, unsettling me. I wanted her to stay out of this. Aldi was right, this was him and me.

"You with this guy?" he slurred. "Hey, girl, he don' work right, he's enemy." He hiccupped. "You all going to cotton out?"

I stood up from the sofa where I was sitting. "Aldi, forget them. They didn't do anything. It's my move. What don't you like?"

I didn't see it coming. Didn't feel a thing. Only the blackness registered. That and the sparkles that had the sensation of a tumble in slow motion. Muffled screams. Shouts. Roar of a crowd from a mile off. I felt his fist hit something soft, then my fist hit his soft. Several times.

A few more thuds, his and mine—his and the other guy's—and time dropped over a cliff…

I forced my eyes open. Find out what's going on. The swirling in my head slowed down. I detected a blur of light. I shut my eyes, not yet ready to see the world. Sounds and words I couldn't make out. Where was I? Nothing came into focus. Waiting for the train to pass. I made an effort to move or thought I did.

"Hey, baby…you okay?"

A soothing sound. Where did it come from? The whirling stopped. I lay on my back staring up at Cynthia. Several people huddled over, across from another huddle over Aldi.

I struggled to get up. A pair of hands helped me sit erect, woozy and nauseous. More hands brought me full height and steered me to a chair.

Cynthia offered me a glass of water. I finished it off, shook my head, and took a deep breath working my jaw to make sure it opened and closed the way it did before. At least I could talk. "Don't tell me. Let me guess," I said, half in jest. "On second thought, tell me, where am I?"

"Right where you were five minutes ago, except in a different universe," Cynthia said. "What do you feel like?"

"I'll be okay. What happened?"

"You guys had a slight disagreement," Ronnie said. "Decided to settle it here and now."

"Who won?"

"You both lost."

Cynthia sat down next to me. I looked up at Ronnie. "Sorry 'bout this, at your birthday bash. I'll set it right."

"Don't worry about it. It's not the first time."

One of the guys I remembered as Jesse grabbed a chair and sat on it in reverse, his arms resting on its back. He addressed no one in particular, which meant everyone. "Right, not the first time an' it won't be the last. Should let white stay white, Black be Black. Better that way."

I hunched forward, elbows on knees, surrounded by a dozen of Ronnie's friends and Cynthia. "What're you saying, Jesse? I didn't pass the test?"

"A for effort, F for results."

"What he's trying to say," Cynthia said with a new edge to her voice, "is some people can't handle it, like Aldi."

"A lot of whites like that," I said. "How to fix it?"

"You tell us."

I looked around the group surrounding me. "What about Cynthia and me? How do we fit into this?"

"It don' matter at all" Dee Dee said. "You like her, she likes you, that's it."

"Not that simple," Tommy G said. "I mean, he's okay, but whites mixin' with Blacks...I dunno. Powerful combustion there."

Dee Dee laughed. "Where'd you learn a word like that?"

"My mammy. Ever time dad farted she'd get on him for his combustion."

A round of laughter eased the tension. Maybe it was a good time to work this out. "Okay, so Cynthia and I get along. We go out, like tonight. Say, I show up again at a party, like this one, and I'm the only white, what then?"

"Depends," Lamont said. "You got a guy like Aldi come along, starts all over again."

"You think I can ever work it out with him?"

"Hard to say. Remember his brother." Lamont thought a moment. "This your first encounter with Black folks?"

"I almost had one with whites." I told them about my trip to New Orleans at the back of the bus. "I didn't feel anything sittin' on the bus."

"Tha's 'cause you was in the driver's seat," Tommy G said. "White people got the numbers, they got the power. Ain't the same."

"There you are. Thas' the whole point," Jesse said. "You say shit, we say what color."

"It's not right," I said. "I never felt that way."

Jesse wagged a finger. "You hain't got our history, slavery an' put down an' all that. How do they say, you hain't walked in our shoes."

I searched for a reply but didn't have one then looked at Cynthia. "What about you? What do you think about us?"

"Maybe Jesse is right about the shoes, but if we stick to that we'll never change. We got to move on, Jesse. Get a new pair. Here's mine," she said, placing her hand on my shoulder.

"Yeah, but you still Black and he be white. Can't change that. Look at it this way. Say, he comes in here, one white and us, what, tweenty Black ones. S'okay. But change the colors. One colored comes in and be with twenty whites. What then?"

"You can't change the color," I said, "but you can change the thinking. Maybe real slow, but ideas don't stay the same."

"Okay," DeAndre said, "I'll go out first thing in the mornin' and get me a white chick. How long you think I last?"

"It don' happen overnight," Dee Dee said.

"Been goin' on for couple of hunnerd years, sister."

"So, who the first Black guy to config with a white woman?" Tommy G said.

"Config?" Where you come up with these words?" Dee Dee said.

"Configuration means to fit together the right way," Tommy G said. "You know, like pieces in a puzzle."

"White and Black is opposites, you dummy," Jesse said. "You config with a white woman, you be hangin' from a tree limb."

I wanted to tell him that Cynthia and me being together put paid to that idea. But I also understood his point.

On the way back to Cynthia's apartment, we went over the evening's altercation and reviewed our own intimacy.

"What do you think?" she asked.

"I'm where you are. Don't care where and don't care who with. Very simple."

"I wish it were that simple." She sat silent as we drove down Washington to Adams. "Anyway, let's try. Be the first of many."

"Can we do it?"

"Why not?"

Over the next several months, Cynthia and I were constant partners, inseparable. Never again did we have a problem, although we steered clear of places we knew were likely to segregate. We weren't out to make a point but would push back if we had to. Sure, there were occasions when someone proved irritating. But we worked it out. Times were changing…perhaps…glacially.

We remained close until our own time ran out. Thing is, unless you're into marriage, experience told me that most relationships last six months to a year. Were they in love?

Maybe not yet but moving in that direction. Then, when I finished my two-year AA at City College, it seemed we'd reached a fork in the road. As close as our relationship had developed, we hadn't made it to the point of forever together. And neither of us wanted to stay in LA.

I had the itch to move on. After studying Chinese for two years, I scratched the itch by getting a berth aboard a Chinese freighter, Asia bound. For her part, Cynthia had contemplated hauling off to Africa where she might practice her newly minted degree in social work.

On our last night, we decided to stay in, to be alone. We talked about the future, telling each other we hoped to reconnect someday, but made no promises. We discussed our relationship, and I agreed that our interracial fling was a life-changing experience. We'd both come to understand the shade of a person's skin is like the proverbial "beauty is only skin deep."

"You really think so?" I said.

"I know so." She paused to draw a needle from the small sewing kit on the nightstand. "Give me your hand."

She pricked my thumb. Then she did the same to hers.

"See, same color."

THE STORY BEHIND THE MYTH
or
THE MYTH BEHIND THE STORY

Southeast Asia, Golden Triangle, 1943-1967

The figure crept through the undergrowth, raced across an open space to the raintree, then clambered up a nearby boulder. It peered over the embankment where only minutes before other figures had met, then scattered. Where were they now?

Hunched down, it listened for any hints of them, ears attuned to distinguish the human from the natural environment: the bark of a dhole dog, the mocking caw of a myna bird, shrieks of snub-nosed monkeys—any sounds of the jungle. Nothing. It meant the others were still close by.

The form, a young boy, crept to another tree, a gnarled old banyan, easy to climb. He scaled up soundlessly, reached a flaring of twisted branches, edged out on one. A favorite vantage point. He waited.

A minute, three minutes, four. There, over by the stand of bamboo, movement, rustling—there they were! The boy broke off a sprig of the banyan's deep red fruit and hurled it to distract their attention. Grabbing a thirty-foot-long liana vine, he rose to his haunches and with a great leap pushed off from the limb to the next tree forty feet away, with a long wild cry ripping away the silence: AAAAEEEEEEE!

Four startled youths looked up, saw the airborne figure swing past them. They broke into a sprint, running, screaming, yelling, toward a large outcrop. One of them tripped, fell, the other three raced on, bounding over the rocky terrain. The flying figure touched ground racing for the same boulder, reached it first, madly scrambled up the flat face, found the summit and turned to face the other three, now four again, just beginning to climb up.

Then all at once, as if prompted by an invisible conductor, the four boys and the lone one, all shirtless wearing only loincloths and shoulder-length hair, laughed and shouted, their taunts raising a bevy of finch and a flock of kites to flutter in the air, until they settled atop a grove of tamarind trees in the distance.

"Yaaah, yaaah, you lost again."

"But you cheated, you didn't say we could use a vine."

"You can use whatever it takes."

The four boys at the bottom stared up at the stocky figure, knowing they'd lost, unwilling to admit it, grudgingly admiring his skills. He *always* won. How come?

"I'm tired of playing," said one. "Let's go swimming. I'll race you."

The other three shouted, turned, and scampered away toward the river. The lone figure squatted down, knees to chin, and watched them scurry over the hard ground, around large rocks, past the towering eucalyptus trees, until he heard screaming and splashing in the water.

According to his birth certificate, issued by an itinerant government official on one of his annual sojourns into Burma's backwoods, ten-year-old Ty Matson was an American, though he'd never been there. Burma was his home where he was born and raised, the son of missionaries from California with the Unity Baptist Church, dedicated to overseas evangelism. Ty's grandfather had started the church and reached British-controlled Rangoon in 1912. Why Abraham chose Burma no one seemed to know. Ty didn't. But if anyone was looking for a challenge, old Abe Matson had found one.

It wasn't the primitive conditions. Any devotee is prepared for that. But mainline Burmese are so devoutly Buddhist, so deeply sacrosanct in their Theravada beliefs, the Baptist preacher might just as well have tried to convert the Pope. Eventually Abraham's son, Jebadiah, assumed leadership of the church. But Jeb and his woman, Bethany, in their search for converts, were forced to move further and further upcountry, away from "civilization." By 1925 they had reached Kengtung in eastern Burma from where they set out to engage the animist minority peoples.

Here Ty's parents settled in, and over the next dozen years, Beth Matson endured eight pregnancies that produced five living children, Ty, the youngest. Since Jeb and Beth were more often than not away from home, traipsing from one isolated village to another, Ty was raised early on by his nanny, a squat, puckish Shan woman who took to the infant like a mother cat to her kittens. Ty never forgot the stern kindness of Nan Thi, and how she used to sneak him special candies and favors when his parents weren't around.

To look at him, Ty Matson seemed like any normal pre-teenager from Chicago or Denver or Seattle: five-foot-six, a hundred-and-thirty pounds, a shock of brown hair dangling over his forehead, a normal appetite for sweets, average in school with a strong preference for romping with his friends. American as apple pie, people who didn't know him said. Maybe. His ma and pa thought otherwise. They kept their thoughts to themselves but watching him shun the other expat kids to play with local native boys knew Ty was anything but the typical American schoolboy.

Early on Ty exhibited the characteristics which later caused him to be dubbed "The Leopard" of which his family had two as pets. His solid frame moved with the feline glide of a cat. He always landed on his feet, never stumbled, never lost his balance. And playing in the jungle had instilled in him a flawless instinct of sensing where danger lurked—ever alert, agile, fluid, like a jungle cat.

The lure of the natural world made it hard to sit still, forever on the move whether at home or "out there" in the wild. His mother often teased him for being the friskiest boy she ever knew. "You rambunctious little rascal. Can't you stay in one place for more'n a minute?" He couldn't.

Ty grew up in Burma's Shan State, cavorting with the different ethnic kids, whether they were Karen or Lahu, Kachin or Wa or numerous others. By the time Ty reached fifteen, he was one of them: could outfox a fox, wrestle a python, track a sambar deer. He once downed a grown 3,000-pound gaur with a blowgun and stopped a wild boar in its tracks with a twelve-inch throwing knife from thirty feet, a skill he learned from his Lahu friends who showed him how to sling it, not from the shoulder but underhand, giving it a flatter trajectory and making it more difficult for a hapless victim to evade. In the middle of all this, he also managed to get some schooling.

When he reached adulthood—for Ty that meant thirteen—he still didn't fit in much with "civilized" society. On Sundays and at special church socials, his parents expected him to mind himself and engage with the sons of other missionaries in the area, or of an occasional visiting diplomat. This, while the adults sipped tea and bit into flaky muffiny things on the spacious lawn that swept down from the two-story mission home. Only his mother's threatening glare kept a rambunctious Ty from stealing away to be with his native buddies. She sometimes scolded him for being unsociable and iconoclastic—words he didn't know the meaning of but he could guess. Secretly, he thought ma kind of took to his rebellious impulses.

But these were issues that barely impinged on young Ty's life. In addition to "jungle jumping" with his friends, he looked forward to going with his parents on their missions, sometimes up north to Lashio or Myitkyina, occasionally over to Laos or Thailand, and a few times even into China. On these sojourns Ty had a chance to explore new places and peoples, to experience a stimulating world of the unusual, the unique, the intriguing—and for Ty, tantalizing.

Early on he learned to identify a tribe from its clothing before confirming it through speech. He knew the Karen preference for striped blues and reds mixed with black, and the Mien—Ty heard some people call them Yao—with their black crisscrossed turbans and thick, red-ruffed collars, the women's tongues keeping pace with flying needles as they practiced their well-known art of embroidery. Lahu women wore ankle-length skirts of red, turquoise, and black bands, with large shiny medallions adorning their chests.

He loved the gaudy Akha, their indigo jackets and knee-length skirts festooned with layers of silver ornaments and glittering regalia. But Ty's favorite were the Lisu, replete with multi-colored strips on their tunics, green-orange-red-blue-white sashes, and streams of silver all crowned by a broad black turban of the same multicolored yarn swirling around and hanging down the back.

Tribal celebrations, which often meant an invitation for the Matson family, thrilled Ty like none he experienced in the toned-down missionary gatherings. The native meetings were lively affairs of music from gongs, drums, and flutes accompanying swaying dancers. Endless chains of food: suckling pigs, green beans with duck eggs, wild cat meat braised in onion and garlic, cauliflower and pork topped with chili and cloves, pickled papaya and lemon grass soup, fried rice mixed with mangoes and duck. And always the pungent odor of anise, ginger, and turmeric slicing the air.

Ty wasn't always sure of what he was eating, but as long as it tasted okay, he didn't care. He didn't even blanche the time a Lahu villager served a special delicacy— sour monkey feces. The concoction from herbivorous simians became a mash of gastric juices the women squeezed out and packed into bamboo tubes to ferment. The resulting grey-green mash they mixed with sour fish paste and served as an hors d'oeuvre.

There were other ponderables in Ty's early experience in Burma, when he first learned about "China White," the ubiquitous opium-cum-heroin found on the steep hillsides of northern Burma, Laos, and Thailand—the Golden Triangle. His father had made it his goal to wean the tribesmen away from the nefarious poppy.

Ty recalled one time when he accompanied his father upcountry. He always looked forward to visiting the Akha, amused with their wood carvings and excited by their giant swings. His father once explained that the Akha originally believed humans and spirits lived together in perfect harmony. But trouble broke out when spirits began stealing chicken eggs from people, and people started taking cucumbers from the spirits. The conflict grew until both sides decided they should live apart— people in villages and spirits in the jungle. In order to separate the human and spirit realms, they built gates at each end of an Akha village. These gates were sacred and protected the village from "all things bad and wicked."

What so titillated young Ty was the carved wooden male and female figures placed by the main gate: the female with a most exaggerated vulva, the male sporting an oversized extended phallus. He grew up thinking the Akha must be the most sexually indulgent people in the world, though his father insisted that they were simply bad craftsmen.

But his father continued to worry about the mind-destroying drugs. On one occasion, a group of black-vested Lahu men sat cross-legged around a fire in front of a large A-frame thatched hut, built on fifteen-foot stilts, the village "meeting place." A blackened tea kettle bubbled over glowing coals. Some of the men smoked thin-stemmed pipes, others chomped on thick Burmese cheroots, a few chewed quids of betel nut, leaning over from time to time to spit streams of pink saliva into the fire. They had sat through a tired monologue from the senior Matson, their impassive faces, Ty sensed, masking a deep concern.

"Your worry is our worry," said Lah Po, the village headman. Ty always wondered how old he really was. His wrinkled, parched, cappuccino skin reminded him of a death-bed patient, but Ty knew how nimble and agile Lah Po was. He could be forty or eighty. "Yes, opium is not a good thing. Some of our own young men seek its happiness, and it brings only sorrow and suffering. And yet—"

"Old wise one," interjected Jebediah Matson, "Our Lord explains that such unnatural things call up the evil spirits. It is for the good of your people if you remove this wicked plant. Let me help you bring new crops—coffee, tea, apple and lichee."

Lah Po held up his hand to interrupt. He had heard this before. "You speak from your heart, honest and truthful. I understand you mean well, as does the Good Lord. But if so, why did the All-Wise One in the sky put the opium poppies here in the first place? Besides, what else will bring in so much income? Nothing. This is our problem."

The inveterate La Poh persisted. "Your words are well-meaning, but we earn much from a small amount of the white powder. It is grown high in the hills and we do not have to share with the lowlanders. It does not spoil. And people who want to buy come to us. If we choose to sell the other crops we must take them down into the valley, and that is much hard work."

Lah Po's reasoning made sense to Ty. He saw both Lah Po's point and his father's view. Hence the dilemma. Lah Po was right. His father was right. Ty had seen many villagers, some his own age, who were addicted, losing all sense of meaning from smoking or eating the concoction. Their emaciated, fever-racked bodies reminded him of decaying cadavers, and he panicked from watching them vomit yellow-green slime from deep in their bowels.

He once tried the drug himself when Kachin friends taunted him to "have some fun." He only remembered the fear he felt at not being able to control his bodily movements, even had trouble standing. And it had brought down on him the wrath of Jebediah Matson which was worse than any opium curse. So even though he sided with Lah Po, Ty grew into an intense foe of China White, especially when he saw its more violent effects.

In the end, his feeling of camaraderie with the natives and the fact that Ty hated the formalities, the hypocrisy of society, called him to the jungles. A free spirit—as his mother said, rambunctious—who believed everybody should be able to do what they wanted, if it didn't hurt anyone. An outlier who understood only the law of the jungle.

Jebediah and Bethany dealt with this the best they could while Ty grew up. But when he turned eighteen and the time came for deciding his future, Jebediah Matson put his foot down and insisted his son have a proper education. What that meant, Ty had no idea. Unfortunately for his father, it meant higher education in the US.

A long-time friend who served as provost at Baylor University in Texas arranged for Ty to begin his college studies, otherwise Ty would never have been accepted. Here he had to forge a new comfort zone. With a heart aching at having to leave his world, and fear of a new reality, Ty packed his bags, bade farewells, and set out for the plains of Texas.

Ty barely squeezed through the first semester. He pined for his former life, felt adrift at the scruffy Waco campus with its white Christian culture. It didn't surprise him at the end of the first term to have to face the dean and listen to Dr. Eakins explain that Ty had failed to carry a "C" average grade. In fact, he might have flunked out had it not been for the "A" he received in ROTC. He had two choices. Study for another semester on probation, during which he must maintain a "B" average lest he be expelled and lose his university exemption and likely be drafted into America's recent foray called the Vietnam War. Or take leave for a year and return in the Fall.

A no-brainer for Ty. Thanking Dr. Eakins, he grabbed his satchel of books, dropped them into a garbage can on his way out, and immediately signed up with the US Marine Corps.

He sailed through boot camp and excelled in the Marine's elite Force Recon training program, including learning to parachute. Then, as soon as he arrived in Vietnam, the Corps notified CIA about his language and open-country skills. Before Ty turned twenty-one he was a Special Forces officer in charge of covert field operations in the tribal border areas ranging over northern Indochina just when the war in Vietnam began hotting up. His exploits soon earned him a reputation few could equal.

Reunited with his home turf, Ty set out to organize bands of local guerilla fighters, especially Lahu and Lisu, at first to engage in hit-and-run raids against Viet Cong and North Vietnamese units wherever he found them. This led him to take on more aggressive action against the traffic along the "Ho Chi Minh trail." Rather than wait for specific orders, he took the initiative to broaden his scope of operations.

He trained mountain tribesmen and sent them on cross-border recon forays as far as China's southern Yunnan Province. And he trained groups of Wa, Chin, and Hmong in a "secret war" in Laos against the Communist Pathet Lao that remained under the radar and therefore unreported.

To anyone else, the life of a lone wolf operating in his own milieu in the midst of an all-out war would have caused his superiors to question his faculties. But Ty basked in his element. He once told a reporter who asked about his life on the edge of civilization. Ty answered with the usual aplomb. "This is where I live, it's my home," he replied, sweeping his arm in a wide arc. "Out there the jungle is a supermarket where I can get anything I want, and it doesn't cost me a penny."

Other stories made the rounds. One concerned his backcountry skills. Trading shots of whiskey with Ty in a Vientiane bar, one reporter asked him about a rumor he'd heard that Ty, with only the clothes on his back, his favorite Bowie knife and a flint, could make his way anywhere in the Triangle for six months, or longer. True or not?

Ty thought a moment, then smiled. "Not quite," he said in his usual soft-spoken manner. "I wouldn't need the flint."

While the war intensified, Ty's area of operation expanded. In 1966, a CIA chopper dropped him into the mountains of central Laos to scout out a suitable site for an airfield closer to Vietnamese and Lao Communist activity along the Ho Chi Minh Trail. Alone and on foot, for several weeks Ty scoured the mountainous, forested terrain until he found an ideal valley near the Plain of Jars. Here he established a base called Long Cheng which eventually turned into the second largest city in Laos. Its 50,000 denizens including local anti-Communist Christians, Lao and NVA turncoat troops, foreign renegades, and a smattering of CIA types maintained an operation with air traffic greater than Chicago's O'Hare.

The key to his success was his intimate knowledge of the area and familiarity with the locals who populated it. Their languages, cultures, and social lives were second nature to him. In addition, his penchant to operate solo allowed him to become a force unto himself without all the layers of "bureaucrazy."

At the same time, his actions built up a mystique of often superhuman exploits. His ethnic troops followed him wherever he went, no questions asked, from battlefield to barroom. His tough and reliable persona easily gained a reputation throughout upper Burma and Thailand, and as far as China.

Like the Pied Piper, the local minority fighters followed him into thick and thin to combat their Communist enemy.

Those who knew him repeated the refrain, "Ty always gets his men out," a motto he turned into gospel and coined a new version, adding women to the mix. He vowed and promised never to abandon anyone who fought with him. "I swear on the Holy Bible and promise never to leave anybody, man or woman, who works for me." Whenever he learned of a fallen or captured comrade, Ty Matson made good his word.

More than once, North Vietnamese soldiers launched series of assaults on CIA strongholds with waves of attackers. The Meo and Hmong defenders mowed down hundreds of the enemy. But the relentless charges continued until only a handful of Ty's original group remained. Most were able to escape during lulls in the fighting. Some accounts say half a dozen fighters were left, others claimed twenty or more. No one knew how many were still alive.

Ty didn't care. He vowed to bring them all down, even if dead. In the end, under a barrage of withering gunfire, he undertook an all-night operation, and with help from a few handpicked devotees—four men and two women—to rescue the entire remaining contingent, scaling the peak six times.

Such exploits created a larger-than-life reputation that reached a point where more and more he overtly challenged CIA strategy. His superiors sensed a loose cannon and questioned his value to the agency. Ty scoffed at the minions from DC, who with their pencil-thin ties and unmussed hair simply did not understand the local customs and sensitivities. "You guys just don't have a feel for the locals. That's why you're losing this war." His animosity for desk jockeys grew, a feeling reciprocated by Washington. As the war in Vietnam ground on, US military leaders and their CIA cohorts sent more and more senior figures to argue policy, and more and more young men and women to die for something, though no one explained to them what it was.

Ty held to his strict understanding of ethnic tribes that winning required tactics based on local beliefs and customs. Not more government bureaucrats and increased fire power. He insisted the newcomers did not understand the local mindset. He scoffed at hearing the new so-called strategy: "Winning hearts and minds." When the CIA eventually relegated him to staff duty, Ty walked.

One afternoon, he left Long Cheng —the same way he had vacated Baylor years before—supposedly to check on supplies, and never returned. The tightknit operation he had worked so successfully soon unraveled while America's strategy of winning those "hearts and minds" turned into body counts. Ty's several thousand combatants disappeared into the hills.

During the years of his forays and missions, the "rambunctious" rascal from Kengtung became a living legend. Over the years, his mother's sobriquet caught on, although the locals and even some foreigners couldn't pronounce it. Eventually people abbreviated the awkward term to a name that caught on for the rest of his life and beyond.

Rambo.

SOULMATE

Northern China, 1985

Another day, another tour group arriving in China from the US to experience the "oldest civilization on earth."

I had left my room at Hong Kong's plush Mandarin Hotel for three weeks of the grime and grunge of China travel. Now I stood in the cavernous waiting room at Beijing's Capitol Airport, packed with shoving hordes, testy and impatient. I held a packet of documents, enough data to identify my group members: names, ages, photos, dietary restrictions if any—always a veggie or two. And medications. I figured most people lied about that, afraid they'd not be allowed to go with the group.

I'd escorted China tours for four years since 1980 and understood all of this. As a tour leader, it was my job to keep everyone satisfied. My MO: size up a group, get a fix on their personalities, and pander to their main interests. Invariably, some individuals forget they can't always have their own way and make incessant personal demands. Early on I learned to counterbalance the group against them—isolate the bad ones.

With half an hour to go, I reviewed the information packet Lindblad Travel provided its tour leaders. A standard bunch. Of the twenty-eight, six came from Canada, two from Mexico. The twenty Americans divided evenly between New Yorkers, and others. I always had mixed feelings about folks from the Big Apple, not all of them, but some. They weren't rude, they simply wanted everything right now and the rest be damned. Those were the worst, the best were much fun to be with.

I checked the overhead arrival board. United 761: delayed. I continued to peruse the manifest. The New Yorkers were traveling as a mini group within a group, as close as "lips and teeth," as the Chinese had it, on a Silk Road tour, advertised to be adventurous and exotic. The promo does not say that it's also grueling.

United 761 has landed. Here they come, traipsing through the crowds until they all gathered around, dazed and bleary-eyed from their twenty-four-hour flights and airport layovers. I checked with Tang, our national guide, to account for their luggage, then boarded the bus for the hotel and a long-anticipated rest.

On this tour, one couple held my interest, Dr. Mortimore Shapiro, 76, neurologist, and Mrs. Anita Ellis Shapiro, 61, vocalist. Mort Shapiro, based on his appearance, hadn't aged well. He acted robust and energetic, just didn't look it. His ungainly demeanor and rumpled attire didn't match my stereotype of a neurosurgeon. Neither did his tired and craggy face, and the sparse head of white hair that seemed permanently uncombed a la Albert Einstein.

By contrast, Anita didn't look or act sixty. She could have been a teenager. Buoyant, affable, lively. Curly black hair. A petite spirited creature. Audrey Hepburn on steroids.

Our five days in Beijing included the regular sites: Great Wall, Forbidden City, Ming Tombs. The day we visited the tombs, the local guide steered the group to Emperor Wan Li's mausoleum, par for the course. It was the most excavated and often the only one visited. And boring. Nothing significant here. Just a huge vacant dungeon. No stories to tell the grandkids.

One China scholar wrote a book on Wan Li's reign (1572-1620), titled *1587, a Year of No Significance*. That pretty much said it all. Spot on.

As our group exercised the tourist shuffle, dragging feet around the dank, impersonal subterranean vault of Wan Li's crypt, I noticed that Anita and Mort seldom moved together. His nuts-and-bolts interests wanted to figure out how the tomb was constructed, questions on design and materials. For Anita, the meaning behind it was paramount. Why was it built, what did it mean? The two went their own ways. When I asked them if they'd like to visit a different tomb, Mort begged off, fixated on how Wan Li's tomb differed from the pyramids. Anita picked up the vibes.

"I'd like you to see a place I think you'll enjoy. Most people miss it."

"Around here?" she said. "What's to miss? There's nothing to see."

"Not quite. Follow me."

We walked a few minutes around several outcrops until we found ourselves cut off from the others. Not another soul around. The seldom-visited tomb itself of the Emperor Yong Lo had yet to be excavated. We approached a palatial foyer that guarded the sepulcher behind it. Like walking into an empty auditorium sans seats, with a silence that demanded awe and respect. The impression you get from entering the Coliseum or Versailles or the Acropolis.

"Oh, my God." Anita remained rooted to the spot. Her gaze swept the expansive courtyard, an enormous, covered terrace supported by gigantic wooden columns.

"How big is this…this galaxy?" she asked, barely able to catch her breath.

I laughed. "You got that right. Over 45,000 square feet."

"What does that mean? Tell me in a way I can understand."

"Think of a football field."

"Oh my God."

She walked to the center and swiveled three-sixty, viewing the area where thirty-two colossal pillars of camphor trees, each forty feet high, supported the roof of yellow-glazed tiles. No nails or screws or brackets. A giant Lego set.

"Each one of these columns comes from a single trunk about five feet thick at the base. It takes three people, arms outstretched, to envelop the entire pillar."

Anita stood as if petrified, then took a few steps to enter the expanse. She reached the nearest column, ran her hands over its polished sheen, as if caressing it.

"What do you think?" I asked.

She didn't hear me, easing through the courtyard, gazing upward at the powerful beams lying horizontal on the pillars, commanding their own domain. Holding her arms wide, she closed her eyes in a pose that reminded me of an evangelical prophet, in tune with the rhythm of the ages, connecting with the past.

"Why this, when the other tombs seem so rigid, so ignoble?" she asked.

"Hard to say, but here's a thought. Every emperor of China of every dynasty, not just the Ming, personally approved and signed off on his own tomb's design and construction. He had to put his imprimatur onto the architecture down to the finest detail. In a way, his tomb reflected his personality. Consider this," I said, gazing upward. "The Yongle emperor had a vision, call it a poetic insight. The world was his to capture. Not militarily, but with an outreach to the peoples of the world."

Anita stood silent. Captured in awe.

"Maybe you've never heard of the great admiral, Cheng Ho. In the early fifteenth century, nearly a hundred years before Columbus, the Emperor Yong Lo ordered him to launch seven naval expeditions to sail the world. It was all so unChinese, to explore the unknown world. Sail the Seven Seas to use a Western reference. This pavilion reflects Yongle's ambition and grandiosity. See for yourself."

In time, Anita came back to the now. "It's magnificent. I love it." She came over to me, gave me a modest hug. "Thank you so much."

After the standard three days of seeing China's capital, we departed by train and passed miles of paddies, ubiquitous peasants bent over, methodically placing rice shoots into slurpy mud in the second phase of replanting, the first being to grow the shoots from seed. The inevitable question came up from the gaggle of curious tourists.

"Oh, look at all those people. What are they doing?"

A legitimate question, but after hundreds of them I gave my now stock sarcastic answer. "Tying their shoelaces."

"Really? I thought they wore sandals."

The train to Xian took the better part of a day. I ended up sitting next to Elizabeth Channing, a close friend of Anita's, who explained to me Anita's professional career.

"She's quite a respected singer in New York. She's played the West Coast, but people outside her circle know her primarily for her dubbing in movies."

"You mean the lip synch business?"

"That's right." She hesitated. "Unfortunately, her inhibitions prevented her from being a super star."

"What happened?" I asked.

"You might talk to her, although she can be touchy about it."

That pretty much put a kibosh to learning anything more.

When we reached China's most popular city, Xian, famous worldwide for its ancient sites, in particular the fabled terra cotta army, I was curious to see how Anita would react to it. Standing on the viewing platform at the head of the massive, enclosed pit, reminiscent of a Boeing hangar, the first sight of this awesome spectacle left a person speechless. Words didn't work. One only stood in disbelief and marveled at the eight thousand clay figures.

I explained some of the particulars to Anita and Mort. "All originally in color, all life-sized. What's more remarkable, each one was *individually* crafted, including distinct facial features, hairdos, and postures. Fingernails, eyelashes, even ear and nose hairs were brushed on. They were produced in parts—head, arms, torso, legs. Same with the horses, though that created a special problem. The body cavities were so large that they couldn't be moved into the kiln to dry. They had to assemble the horse inside the oven or build the kiln around it in order to bake the piece."

That got Mort really going. He took off, his four cameras dangling from shoulders and around his neck, wanting to capture everything on film, and then some.

Anita exemplified the feeling and emotional side of life. Gazing over the spectacle left her short of words.

"Oh, my God." It had become a refrain.

I watched her taking it all in. Not thinking as her husband did, but feeling, absorbing this immensity of human vision and creation.

"Why did they do this?" she asked. Again, the why.

"No one's quite sure. What do you think?"

I watched her struggle to gain an understanding. "I think whoever made this happen either had a great vision, or a great ego."

"Probably both. Or a great fear."

Continuing to gaze at the scene, she asked, "Fear of what? This doesn't look like anything done by a person who's afraid."

"Of uncertainty. Of the future. Of life after death. Some scholars say it was to assure the emperor a safe journey into the afterlife. Kind of an insurance policy into the unknown. He wanted to command not only all under heaven, as the Chinese put it, meaning the entire world as they saw it, but heaven itself." I stopped to consider Anita's reasoning. "I can also accept he was a visionary. And we know through historical records, an egotistical monster."

"Who is 'he'?"

"His birth name was Ying Jeng, but the Chinese refer to him as the First Emperor, the first person to unify a dozen squabbling states into an empire, in the third century BC.

He called his empire Chin. That's where the word 'China' comes from."

"Incredible," she said, turning to walk around the entire pit.

Following the singular experiences of Yung Lo's tomb in Beijing and the First Emperor's army, we headed due west into Xinjiang province, giving up trains for buses when scrub gave way to desert dunes. We lumbered along two-lane roads, fifty miles between towns, forcing us to make unscheduled pit stops. Since the only thing in sight was a vast desert, our only solution was to separate men and women to either side of the road and turn our backs.

Our destination this time was Dunhuang, the major outpost along the old Silk Road, over a thousand years ago. An oasis-turned-entrepot in ancient China filled with itinerants of every sort: traders, merchants, pilgrims, mercenaries, imperial troops—and the women who accompanied them. We'd reached the outer fringe of cosmopolitan China, where local minorities—Uyghurs, Kazaks, Kirgiz, Tatars, and other Turkic-speaking peoples—outnumbered the Han Chinese. Demographically, we were no longer in China.

The highlight here was the Mogao grottoes, a Buddhist homeland. A series of over seven hundred caves, two thousand statues, and tens of thousands of square feet of murals. We had two days to take in what would require months to see everything, and which would turn to complete boredom for all but the most fervent specialist. After a couple of hours, I asked Anita if she'd like to check out a different venue.

She laughed. "You know me by now. Let's go."

I took her past the long line of caverns and queued-up tourists until we reached the last cave, then continued for several minutes along a path that most people didn't know about, circling around until we climbed to a higher level well above the grotto complex. We scrambled up a steep rise and found ourselves standing on top of the world.

Anita: "Oh, my God."

We stepped forward, toward the distant mountains a million miles off, shimmering from heat distortions created by the rising hot air. A few hundred yards out, we stopped to contemplate the immensity around us. I don't know if "absolute silence" is possible, but we were close.

We stood for a few minutes, choosing not to say anything. Finally, without looking at her, I asked, "What are you thinking?"

She hesitated. "I feel so insignificant. I wonder if it makes any sense to say that everything is nothing. I can't describe it, it's mystical. Makes me want to sing."

"Do it. No one's around."

She shook her head. "I can't. It doesn't seem right."

I forced myself not to ask why.

We drank in the immensity until I heard our guide call the group to return to the bus. Aboard, he reminded us of our early morning departure for the all-day ride to Urumchi. The next day, rambling through the desert of the Gansu Corridor—an extension of the Gobi—I sat with Anita, wanting to learn more about her professional life.

"How many times have people asked about your ghost singing for movies?"

She smiled. "So, you talked to Elizabeth."

"She did mention it."

"That's okay, she means well. My problem is that once the information gets out, everyone wants me to sing. They've kept after me for most of the trip. But I just can't do it. Elizabeth must have mentioned my limitation."

"Very briefly. She really didn't say much."

She paused, as if pondering what to reply. "You know, I'm plagued with stage fright, I've never been able to get past it. I can't perform in front of an audience."

"I've heard of stage fright, but that sounds pretty severe."

"It's not just stage fright, it's more than that. It's a crippling. It kept me from exercising my own gifts, stopped me cold. A total lack of control in front of people, even on a movie set. Not only can I not sing, I can't find the words. I freeze, turn into a statue."

"What about your recordings?"

"I'm okay with technicians around, it's the room full of people staring at me that I can't take. For instance, I never sang with a band. Thinking about a crowd puts me in traction."

"Did you get any help, or just gut it out?"

She stopped to open a bottle of water and drank several gulps. "I get so dry out here," she said, wiping her lips. "For a while I did try to brave myself through. Dug in my heels, all that sort of thing. Nothing worked. When I was in my mid-30s, I went with my mother to a psychiatrist. My mother, you know, was a beautiful singer of popular songs, but only at home. My father didn't think it right for a woman to sing in public, so he didn't allow my mother to perform. The doctor said, because of my father's domineering behavior, I must have told myself, if I sing in public, I'll lose a man's love, and I'll lose my parents' love."

That pushed me back. "Pretty heavy diagnosis. Once you learned the reason for your problem, what happened?"

She shook her head. "Even with that insight, I couldn't overcome what I call my paralysis."

"What did you do then?"

"I love to sing, I feel like I want to pay homage to song. That's when I turned to dubbing for others, in the movies."

"Which ones?"

"Do you know the picture 'Gilda,' with Rita Hayworth?"

"One of my favorites. Her torch song, 'Put the Blame on Mame' brought the house down. You sang that?"

She nodded. "That wasn't Rita singing, it was me."

"It's hard to believe it wasn't Rita. Was her voice that bad?"

"In fact, she had a very nice voice. She wanted to do the song herself. But Harry Cohn, head of Columbia Pictures, always dubbed her because it was cheaper. He'd have to pay her ten times what he paid me. Rita was such a good lip syncer, nobody knew it wasn't her voice until many years later. In fact, I dubbed for her in four other films, including "Pal Joey."

"Did you dub for anyone else?"

"A few. Vera Ellen, Shelly Winters, Joan Caulfield, Jeanne Crain, among others."

"That's amazing. When you work with them, how do you approach the song? I mean, do you study the woman on the screen, say Rita in her nightclub act? Or do you think about what the movie's about, or what the song is about? There must be a lot of psychology in it."

She thought for a moment. "Something like that. I work on my interpretations by considering the subtext that's related to the lyric. I look for what the scene calls for, and what the lyricist and composer want. You can call it a single-handed collaboration. I'll compare notes with the actor, but in the end it's my call."

"That's a lot of work," I said.

Our guide interrupted to tell us we'd arrive at the hotel in a few minutes.

"Okay, thanks Tang." I looked at Anita. "I hope to hear you someday."

She squeezed my hand. "Come to New York."

"I'll be there." I excused myself to check our group into the hotel.

After so many magnificent and inspiring sights, Urumchi was a letdown. The sole reason for going there was to catch one of the three-a-week return flights to Shanghai. Due to scheduling, we had to stay in Urumchi for two nights, one too many. Then I checked my passenger docs and found that the second and final night was Anita's birthday.

Lindblad had a standing practice to observe people's birth dates. So, to liven things up, I ordered a gala bash for Anita's. In fact, it was to be a simple but special dinner and cake, a gift, and a hail-and-hearty send-off. That was the extent of Urumqi's entertainment venue.

After eighteen days on the move without a break, people were run-down. Cranky. Short-tempered. Impatient. It was especially hard on Anita who had continuously to fend off requests for her to perform. The more they kept at it, the more she resisted, trying to say a nice "no," and not always so nice.

Nothing was scheduled for our final day except the farewell dinner, so everyone visited the local bazaar for its tourist trinkets. I found a shop with some decent jewelry. I picked a pendant and had her name inscribed in Chinese. The group came together and contributed a generous present of over $500 and wondered what to do with it. Some didn't like the idea of giving money, so in the end, Tang and I negotiated a colorful hand-woven silk carpet, including the postage to send it to the Shapiro's home in New York. I also ordered a special silver pendant inscribed with her name in Chinese, A-ni-ta.

I asked Tang about a special restaurant to have a party. He told me the hotel was the best in town. When he took me to the dining hall, my heart sank. It reminded me of an empty ballroom, as exciting as an art gallery without the art. It had all the cachet of a prison. Still, the hotel staff was good enough to string up banners and bunting, hoping to create a festive atmosphere, enhanced by several tables of other foreign tourists, maybe a hundred people all told.

The combination of tired camaraderie, end-of-tour relief, and endless bottles of Wild Goose Beer—one wag wondered if that was a noun or a verb—put us all in a good mood. China's infamous Maotai white lightning made from sorghum ratcheted it up. Anita didn't drink, but she fell into the usual hail-fellow-well-met atmosphere.

After some of the group gave her small mementos like mine, Mort complied when I asked him to present the silk carpet to his wife. This had an enormous impression on her. She sat dumbfounded. "Oh, my God!"

Anita's reaction left a feel-good atmosphere over the group.

I knew everyone would sit back for one last round, then head for their quarters to prepare for the next morning's flight to Shanghai, and homeward. I glanced at Anita who wore an odd expression. She seemed in a fog, as if she wasn't with us anymore. I started to worry.

I was on the point of asking if she felt all right when she stood, almost zombie-like, and walked off about twenty feet toward the center of the hall. Everyone, our group and the others, fell silent, watching.

Not a sound, the Chinese attendants shushed.

Anita stood quiet and still, eyes closed. Then, in the center of a cavernous room with the acoustics of an echo chamber, she eased into an a cappella rendition of Rogers and Hart's "Wait Till You See Him." Hard to describe, a cross between honey and silk, a clear-as-a bell sexy purr. Like an endless sonic carpet. Her vibrato caromed off the walls.

When she finished, all hundred or so people in the room, Chinese and foreigners alike, jumped up and broke out in a crescendo of applause. I heard Elizabeth, sitting next to me, "Oh, my God."

When the clapping eased up, Anita/Rita launched into Rita's signature song, "Put the Blame on Mame." This pint-sized powerhouse of vocal dynamite swam through the stanzas, her voice undulating to create and sustain the energetic, sensuous, voluptuous mood the song demands. I swear I felt Rita in the room with us.

For a second time, Anita brought the house down.

Back in "civilization," in Shanghai, I accompanied the group to Capitol Airport. Tang stayed with the majority, while I went with Mortimore and Anita to the Pan Am counter to check them into their first-class seats. They grabbed their carry-ons and headed for immigration. Mort moved ahead, yacking with others from our group, probably wondering how the airport was constructed. Anita held back, and we chatted for a couple of minutes. She said what a wonderful experience

she and M⸱⸱ ⸱ad had. Then, she reached into her bag and
pulled ⸱⸱ ⸱n LP album, her latest release, "A Legend Sings,"
hug⸱⸱⸱ ⸱e ⸱nd bussed me on the cheek.
⸱⸱⸱th this, maybe you'll remember our special time. It's
⸱ wonderful. I'll never forget it. Take care."
She turned and walked away. Once I lost sight of her, I
⸱ooked at the album cover where she'd inscribed the following:

Anita Kert Ellis d⸱⸱⸱⸱ ⸱⸱⸱ 2015,
at ⸱⸱⸱

she and Mort had had. Then, she reached into her bag and pulled out an LP album, her latest release, "A Legend Sings," hugged me and bussed me on the cheek.

"With this, maybe you'll remember our special time. It's been wonderful. I'll never forget it. Take care."

She turned and walked away. Once I lost sight of her, I looked at the album cover where she'd inscribed the following:

For Allen,
My soulmate in adventure
and love of nature.
All my love,
Anita Ellis

Anita Kert Ellis died on October 28, 2015,
at the age of 95.